Also by the Author

The Devil You Know

The Erin O'Reilly Mysteries
Book Thirteen

Steven Henry

Clickworks Press • Baltimore, MD

First publication: Clickworks Press, 2021
Release: CWP-EOR13-INT-P.IS-1.0

Sign up for updates, deals, and exclusive sneak peeks at clickworkspress.com/join.

Ebook ISBN: 978-1-943383-79-5
Paperback ISBN: 978-1-943383-80-1
Hardcover ISBN: 978-1-943383-81-8

For Greg Hewett, my college English professor,
who helped me find my voice.

The Devil You Know

To make the syrup, combine 1 cup pomegranate juice, 1/3 cup honey, 1 tbsp. dried oolong tea leaves, 1 tbsp. dried green tea leaves, 1 tsp. cracked black pepper, and the peel of 1 lemon in saucepan. Bring to boil over medium-high heat. Reduce heat to medium-low for 15 minutes. Cool and strain into glass container. Makes 1-1 ¼ cups of syrup. Cover and refrigerate syrup until needed.

To make the drink, muddle 4 slices of fresh ginger root with ½ oz. lime juice in a cocktail shaker. Add 1 ½ oz. tequila, ½ oz. green Chartreuse, and 1 oz. of syrup. Shake vigorously and pour into a Collins glass filled with crushed ice. Carefully pour ½ oz. mescal so it floats on top. Garnish with a ginger slice and lemon twist and serve.

Chapter 1

Erin O'Reilly stared at the painting on the museum wall. She didn't know much about art, though she'd once held a painting worth millions of dollars. The painting in front of her wasn't for sale, had never been appraised. But it hung here in the Guggenheim, in the heart of Manhattan, in a place of honor, so it had to be worth something.

The artist hadn't used the traditional oil on canvas of so many masters. This painter had opted for watercolors on some sort of heavy paper. A commentary on the impermanence of everything, even art? She'd heard Tibetan monks liked to make pictures out of colored sand, which blew away in the next strong wind.

Erin peered closer, trying to decipher the image. She saw eyes, big blue ones with cartoonishly enlarged curled lashes, atop a toothy grin so white it suggested very good dental care. The background was yellow, which she thought of as a happy color.

"Auntie Erin?"

Erin became aware of a tugging on the leg of her slacks. She looked down to see her niece, one hand curled into the fabric, the other poking meditatively into the corner of the girl's mouth.

"What's up, kiddo?" she asked.

"I'm bored."

Erin dropped to one knee so they were eye to eye. "Why's that?"

"We're in a museum," Anna said.

"So?"

"Museums are bo-ring." The nine-year-old stretched the word out as far as it would go.

"Look at this stuff," Erin said. "These things were all made by kids, some of them your own age. Now they're hanging here for grown-ups to look at, just like any artist. Isn't that neat?"

"I guess, but I've seen them. Now I'm bored."

Erin smiled. She supposed the Guggenheim's annual Year with Children exhibit was something a girl Anna's age might soon tire of. She ruffled the kid's hair affectionately.

"Look, you still want to be a cop when you grow up?"

"I'm going to be a detective just like you," Anna said in tones of absolute certainty.

"You know, detectives spend a lot of time on stakeouts. Do you know what that is?"

"Yeah. When you sit in your car waiting to catch the bad guys."

"Exactly. And do you know what we do while we wait for them?"

Anna thought about it. She shook her head.

"We just sit, usually in the dark," Erin said. "For hours. You have to learn to be patient."

Anna considered this. "What do you do when you have to go potty?" she asked with a pre-teen's practicality.

"We hold it. Or we use an empty paper cup."

"Really? Eww!" Anna wrinkled her nose. "But you can't get out of your car for anything?"

"If we did, the bad guys might see us," Erin explained. "So we just have to wait. Like you and I have to wait for your mom and brother."

"But you get food while you wait, right?" Anna asked.

"Yeah, we eat in the car."

"I want ice cream," Anna declared.

"I haven't got it in my pockets, kiddo," Erin said.

"Ice cream," Anna said again, crossing her arms. "If we're on stakeout, I want ice cream."

"You're going to end up a union rep for sure," Erin said. "They'll like a negotiator like you. Tell you what. We'll go looking for your mom and Patrick. When we find them, I'll ask about the ice cream. If your mom says it's okay, then we can have it."

"Yaaay!" Anna said. She grabbed Erin's hand and tugged enthusiastically.

They found Michelle O'Reilly and Patrick in the next room, in front of a display of clay sculptures that looked like fluorescent-colored dinosaurs of some sort. Patrick was trying to reach past his mother to get his hands on one of them. Michelle was trying to steer him clear of the display. So far it seemed to be a draw.

"I've got a vote for ice cream," Erin announced.

"Oh, thank God," Michelle said. "Sean wanted another kid. I should've talked him into a pet squirrel instead. It'd be less work. Let's go." Patrick, seeing her momentary distraction, tried to slip past her. Michelle, without even looking, snared him with a deft forearm and scooped him up into her arms. He wriggled, trying to escape, and she tickled him. He was soon reduced to helpless squeals.

"Motherhood, huh?" Erin said as Anna pulled her toward the exit and Michelle followed, still carrying the youngest O'Reilly.

"It's the greatest gift a woman can have," Michelle said. "Or so everyone keeps telling me." But she was smiling. Michelle was a tall, strikingly attractive woman a few years older than Erin. She'd married Erin's brother, a trauma surgeon at Bellevue Hospital, and bucked the conventional wisdom of the twenty-first century by deciding to be a housewife and mother. She'd spent this morning with her kids and her sister-in-law the Major Crimes detective.

"Anna got bored," Erin explained in an undertone.

"Are you kidding?" Michelle said. "This is the most excitement I've had all week."

"Excitement isn't all it's cracked up to be," Erin said. "Just be glad you're not tripping over dead bodies all day."

"It does put my life in a little perspective," Michelle said. "My husband spends his time saving lives, his sister catches killers, and I go to PTA meetings."

"You've got a couple of great kids," Erin said.

"I know," Michelle said, still smiling. "I guess the grass is always greener."

It was a good couple of blocks to the nearest supermarket, on Madison Avenue, but it was a pleasant, sunny day and Anna's energy carried them along. Erin was enjoying her day off, though she missed her partner. Her K-9, Rolf, was back at Michelle and Sean Junior's Midtown brownstone, hopefully having a nice nap.

"How's your boyfriend?" Michelle asked.

"He's doing well," Erin said. "He can get around a lot better now. They say he's going to make a full recovery."

It was still a little strange to be openly talking to her family about her boyfriend. She and Morton Carlyle had kept their relationship secret right up until a would-be assassin had shot him in the stomach in the middle of Erin's living room. After that, things had gotten complicated. Carlyle was a gangster,

Erin was a cop, and the two of them were trying their best to thread their way through the obstacle course their love life had become. Carlyle was ostensibly working for the NYPD now as an informant, but it would be a while before they accumulated enough evidence to move on his associates in the O'Malley mob. In the meantime, Erin figured she'd take a quiet, sunny day with the family. It beat getting shot at.

"I still need to meet him," Michelle said.

"Soon," Erin promised.

"I hate that word," Anna said.

"Why?" Erin asked.

"When grown-ups use it, it means the same thing as 'never,'" Anna said.

"Smart kid," Erin remarked to Michelle.

* * *

Armed with Magnum ice cream bars, they emerged from the supermarket a quarter of an hour later. They started in the direction of Central Park. The plan was to get hot dogs from a cart somewhere along the way and have a picnic lunch.

"Life is uncertain," Michelle said. "Sometimes you should eat dessert first."

"Mommy?" Anna said in muffled tones.

"Don't talk with your mouth full, dear," Michelle said automatically.

"Mommy, that lady looks sick," Anna said, pointing.

"Don't stare and don't point," Michelle said. "It's rude."

Erin, as a police officer, had different standards of etiquette than civilians. Anything out of the ordinary was worth her attention, and she didn't care if someone thought she was staring. She followed Anna's gesture.

A blonde woman was weaving her way along the sidewalk.

Her high-heeled, knee-high boots weren't made for stability and she kept stumbling. Her face was a ghastly smear of day-old makeup, scarlet lipstick painting a gash across her pale features. Her hair was a tangled mess of curls. Her eyes were hollow and staring, with pupils that belonged on another planet.

"She's not sick," Erin said quietly.

"Is she on drugs?" Anna asked loudly.

Michelle winced. But even though the blonde was less than twenty feet away, the other woman gave no sign that she'd heard.

"It's not even noon," Michelle muttered out of the side of her mouth. "You'd think she'd have the decency not to get hammered this early."

Erin had seen drunk or strung-out people at every hour of the day or night. Chemical dependency didn't operate on a nine-to-five schedule. But this woman looked harmless enough. The blonde was dressed for a wild night. Her long legs were clad in fishnet stockings that ran up under a very short miniskirt. Her halter-top was only barely decent. She looked like a hooker, and not an expensive one.

The blonde teetered past the O'Reillys. Then, abruptly, she swerved off the curb and stumbled into the street.

Erin's police instincts kicked in even before the first blare of a car horn. Her half-eaten ice cream bar fell from her hand and splattered on the concrete. She was sprinting toward the woman by the time the ice cream hit the ground. A white panel truck laid rubber on Fifth Avenue, fishtailing and trying to swerve out of the way.

Erin grabbed the woman's arm and yanked as hard as she could. The blonde, off-balance, tumbled toward her. They fell back together onto the curb. Erin felt a sharp pain in her side where the concrete dug into her. The truck continued on its way with a last irritable blast of its horn.

"What the hell were you thinking?" Erin snapped.

"Sorry," the blonde mumbled. "Couldn't... tell... where'm I?"

"Downtown Manhattan," Erin said grimly, getting to her feet. She saw her family coming toward her and waved them back. "You could've been killed."

"Sorry," the woman said again, and Erin saw she was scarcely more than a girl under the caked-on makeup.

"What's your name?" Erin asked.

"Tammy." The girl sat on the curb and hugged her elbows.

"What are you doing out here, Tammy?"

"Looking..."

"Looking for what?"

Tammy squinted at Erin, trying to focus. "Help," she said, shaping her lips carefully and distinctly around the word.

"You need help?" Erin asked. She reached into her hip pocket and pulled out her gold shield. "It's okay. I'm a detective. What do you need help with?"

"Not for me," Tammy said. "For him."

"Who?"

"Man... in the car."

"What man? What car?"

"Nice car. Fancy."

"Did a man in a nice car do something to you?" Erin asked. This was looking like a potential sexual assault case.

"Don't... remember."

"Where is the man?"

"In the car."

"Where's the car?"

Tammy waved her hand vaguely back the direction she'd come from.

"Were you in the car?" Erin asked.

Tammy nodded.

"Do you know this man?" Erin pressed.

"Don't know. Don't think so. Head... hurts." Tammy pressed a hand against her forehead.

"Why does he need help?"

"I think... think he's... dead."

Chapter 2

"I need you to think hard, Tammy," Erin said. "I need you to take me to the car with the man in it. Can you do that?"

She glanced around. Except for Michelle, Anna, and Patrick, nobody was taking the slightest notice of them. Here they were, on a crowded street in the middle of the biggest city in America, talking about a dead man, and no one cared. Typical.

Tammy scrunched up her face. "Black," she said.

"What's black?" Erin asked, telling herself to be patient.

"What's Auntie Erin doing?" Anna asked her mother.

"Her job," Michelle said.

"But it's her day off," Anna said.

"Black car," Tammy said. "Black man. Red eyes."

"Stand up," Erin said. She managed to steer the unsteady woman to her feet. "Now let's go find this guy."

Tammy teetered along the sidewalk, Erin holding her lightly by the upper arm in case the girl decided to take another header into the street. Michelle and the kids followed at a discreet distance.

They walked up Fifth Avenue along the east border of Central Park. The city buzzed with life on all sides. Erin felt a sense of eerie unreality. Death wasn't unusual in public places in New York, but it was usually accompanied by screams, the sound of cars crashing into each other, and a prompt police response.

Tammy was disoriented and confused. She paused and looked both ways. "I thought..." she said. "Oh. There it is."

She lunged for the street. If Erin hadn't held her back, Tammy's secrets would have died under the wheels of a Chevy Tahoe.

"How about we go to that crosswalk?" Erin suggested, pointing her up the street.

"Erin, maybe you should call someone," Michelle said.

"I'm the one they call, Shelley," Erin said. "This might not be anything. But get your phone ready. And keep the kids back, unless you want to be paying for a few years of therapy."

"What's she talking about, Mom?" Anna asked.

Erin and Tammy crossed Fifth Avenue. Tammy raised a hand and pointed with one badly-painted scarlet fingernail. Erin looked along the extended digit and saw a black Mercedes parked on the street. Its rear passenger door was standing a few inches open.

"Stay right here," Erin told Tammy. "Sit down by this wall. Don't move." Then she advanced on the car, coming up from behind.

The windows were heavily tinted. She couldn't tell who, or what, might be inside. Her hand dropped automatically to her hip, but she'd left her service sidearm at home. However, Erin O'Reilly wasn't about to be caught unarmed, even on a museum trip with her brother's kids. She dropped into a crouch and came up with her ankle gun, a snub-nosed .38 revolver. It was useless outside twenty-five feet or so, but at close range it was as good as any pistol. Holding the revolver in one hand, she angled in on the Mercedes's open door.

"NYPD," she said. "Anyone in there, keep your hands where I can see them."

The car sat silent and unmoving.

Erin reached out with her free hand, being careful not to touch any surface likely to have fingerprints, and levered the door the rest of the way open. She stepped back at once, covering the vehicle's interior.

The sour smell of vomit, all too familiar to any Patrol cop, wafted out to meet her. In the Mercedes's dome light, she saw a figure slumped in the back seat. It was a man, more or less dressed in a rumpled suit. His coat hung open, unbuttoned. His necktie was untied and trailed loose. And most notably, his pants and boxers were down around his ankles.

"Sir?" Erin inquired, bending closer. He looked like a younger guy, probably in his mid-twenties. The suit was expensive, probably custom-tailored. She saw the glitter of diamonds on his cufflinks. His skin was a bluish purple under a surface pallor. He wasn't breathing.

"Shelley, call 911," Erin said over her shoulder. "Right now." While her sister-in-law dialed, Erin bent inside the car. One of the man's arms lay across the seat. She picked up the hand and felt the inside of the wrist, looking for a pulse. His skin was cool to the touch. The fingernails were such a dark purple they looked black.

"No pulse," Erin muttered. And with the body temp so low, he'd been dead a while. She looked more closely at the young man's face. His lips were the same color as his nails. A thin trail of yellow bile ran down from the corner of his mouth. His silk shirt was stained with dried vomit.

Erin had been wearing a shield for twelve years. Dead bodies had long ago ceased to hold any terror for her. She reached up to his face and pushed open an eyelid. The pupil was contracted to a pinpoint of black. His eye was a bright blue that might have been attractive in other circumstances.

A siren cut the air with its shrill wail, very close by. Erin heard the screech of tires and a pair of car doors opening behind her. She pulled out her shield and got out of the car, holding the gold detective insignia up so it was the first thing the other cops saw. The last thing she wanted was to take friendly fire from some overeager rookie.

Two uniformed NYPD officers ran toward her. "What've we got?" the older one asked.

"One body in the car," she said, holstering her pistol. "Looks like an overdose. You got naloxone? I think he's a goner, but we might as well try."

"Your lucky day," he replied. "Riviera, grab the OD kit."

The other cop sprinted back to his car. His partner hurried to meet Erin. "Sergeant Nelson," he introduced himself.

"O'Reilly, Major Crimes," Erin replied. "We can try the naloxone, but I think it's too late." Naloxone was a wonder drug, only recently approved for use. It could, if administered quickly enough, counteract an opioid overdose. Erin had heard it could do near-miraculous things, but it couldn't bring a man back from the dead.

Nelson peered into the Mercedes. "Whew," he whistled. "How long's he been like this?"

"Don't know," she said. "That girl over there brought me here."

Tammy was sitting against the park wall, just as she'd been told. Slowly, almost delicately, she bent over and threw up on the ground.

"Nice witness," Nelson commented. "Good and reliable."

Riviera rejoined them. The younger cop was fumbling with the squad car's emergency gear, pulling out a syringe.

"You know how to use that?" Nelson asked.

"Sure thing, Sarge," Riviera said.

"Do it."

Riviera climbed into the back seat and plunged the syringe into the man's arm. "Chest compressions?" he suggested.

"No point," Nelson said. He looked at Erin. "If it's heroin and the naloxone doesn't work, he's toast. You sure it's a drug overdose?"

"Classic symptoms," she said.

"Yeah," he agreed. "I've worked Street Narcotics. I've seen it before. A guy OD's on H, you got one to three hours, tops, before he's done. What's his skin temp?"

"Cool," Erin said, remembering the clammy flesh under her fingertips.

Nelson shook his head. He keyed the radio clipped to his shoulder. "This is Fourteen Delta. We need a bus at Fifth Avenue and 87th. Got a 10-54U, probable opioid OD, unresponsive."

"No vitals, Sarge," Riviera reported, getting back out of the car. "Naloxone didn't do jack. I think he's gone."

"Figured," Nelson sighed. "This a homicide, Detective?"

"Beats me," Erin said.

"You caught the body," he said. "What's Major Crimes want this guy for?"

"We don't," she said. "I'm off-duty. I just ran into that girl and she asked for help."

"No such thing as off-duty," Nelson replied. "But if that's the situation, we can take it from here. I'll get a statement from the girl. Probably just some rich idiot who partied too hard. We got an ID on him?"

"Not yet," Erin said. "You got an extra pair of gloves?"

"Sure thing, Detective," Nelson said, producing a roll of disposable gloves from a back pocket. "You didn't bring your own?"

"I was taking my niece and nephew out for ice cream," she

said, pulling the gloves on. "Sorry I didn't think to bring an evidence kit."

She climbed into the back seat once again. In a way, having the guy's pants down was easier. She could check his pockets with no trouble. She felt the bulge of a wallet in his hip pocket.

"Bingo," she said, fishing it out. She flipped open the expensive leather to find a driver's license. She also saw dollar bills and credit cards. He hadn't been robbed.

"Who was he?" Nelson asked.

Erin shrugged. "Martin Ross. That name mean anything to you?"

"Nah," Nelson said.

"Hey, Sarge," Riviera said. "Isn't he that politician's kid? You know, Senator Ross?"

"Huh?" Nelson said. "Wait a second, you mean Marcus Ross?"

"Yeah," Riviera said. "I saw the kid in one of those tabloid papers. You know, like they got at grocery checkout counters. He was in some kind of scandal earlier this year."

Erin and Nelson looked at him.

"What?" Riviera said defensively. "My wife reads them."

"I'll bet," Erin said, grinning. "So this is a state senator's son?"

"Looks like it," Nelson said. "You sure Major Crimes doesn't want a piece of this?"

"I'm sure we don't want it," she said. "But we'll probably end up with it."

She hated politics.

*   *   *

Erin didn't get her hot dog after all. She sent Michelle and the kids on to Central Park, while she stayed at the scene. Anna gave her a hug.

"Catch the bad guys," the girl said.

"I'll try," Erin said, wondering if there even were bad guys in this situation.

The EMTs arrived fast, but no response time would have saved Martin Ross. He was pronounced dead at the scene, to no one's surprise. He'd been gone for a couple of hours, according to the medics' estimate.

The paramedics moved on to Tammy, while Erin and the uniformed officers kept the growing crowd of bystanders back. Another squad car arrived for perimeter duty. Several New Yorkers were busily recording the whole thing on their phone cameras, and soon enough a news van showed up. The whole thing was turning into sidewalk theatre. The cops ignored the reporters.

"What do you think?" Erin asked one of the paramedics, walking over to see how they were doing with her witness.

"Opioid," the EMT said without hesitation. "Heavy dose. But she's coming off it okay. She'll be fine."

"Sleepy," Tammy said. Her eyes were closed. She swayed from side to side. The medic caught her before she could tip over.

"Does she need a hospital?" Erin asked.

"I don't think so," he said. "Just throw her in the drunk tank and let her come down on her own."

"We can take her back to the One Nine if you want," Sergeant Nelson suggested. "Which precinct are you?"

"I'm at the Eightball," Erin said. "I think we better go through your station, since this happened in your backyard."

"Our crap, our problem," he agreed. "But our morgue is on the fritz. Wiring problem. We've been sending our bodies to Bellevue for a couple days."

"That's fine," she said. "I can call our ME and have her swing by the hospital."

"What do you want to do with her?" Nelson asked, pointing a thumb Tammy's direction.

"Talk to her. Find out what she knows."

"Here, or back at the One Nine?"

Erin considered. She looked around at the crowd of civilians. "Let's go to your house," she decided. "She needs a little more time to sober up, and I'd rather not do an interview that's going to end up on some rubbernecker's web page."

Then she took out her phone. She had to make a couple of calls. The first was to her commanding officer.

"Webb," the Lieutenant said.

"It's O'Reilly, sir. I've got a body."

There was a short pause. "O'Reilly," Webb said slowly, "I think we may need to go over the concept of a day off again. You don't seem to have grasped it."

"I didn't go looking for it," she said. "I was out with the family. It just fell into my lap."

"Where are you?"

"Fifth Avenue and 87th. I'm with some uniforms from the One Nine. We've got a witness I'd like to interview. If it's okay, I'll do it at their station."

"Fine with me," Webb said. "Homicide?"

"I don't think so. Drug overdose, from the looks of it."

"That's a Narcotics case, not Major Crimes."

"Yes, sir. I'll just make sure there's no funny business and hand it off to their Narcs."

"Why would there be funny business?"

"You know Marcus Ross, sir?"

"State Senator Ross? Of course I do. He's up for re-election this fall. Oh Lord, he's not dead, is he?"

"His son, I think."

Webb was silent for ten very long seconds. "You know the

official policy, don't you?" he said at last.

"What policy is that, sir?"

"Every death counts the same. We investigate every one equally."

"Of course."

"And you know the official policy is bullshit," Webb added. "Some count more than others."

"Yes, sir."

"Be careful on this, O'Reilly."

"Yes, sir."

"And try not to get Major Crimes involved, unless there actually is a major crime. Am I clear?"

"Yes, sir."

"O'Reilly?"

"Yes, sir?"

"When you keep saying that, it makes me very suspicious."

Erin smiled. "I'll be careful, sir. O'Reilly out."

Then she dialed Sarah Levine.

"Precinct 8 Medical Examiner," Levine answered.

"Hey, Doc, it's Erin O'Reilly. Can you get to Bellevue Hospital?"

"Given normal traffic patterns and absent extreme weather abnormalities, it's definitely possible," Levine said.

"Right. Please go there when you get the chance. I'm sending a body down, probable heroin overdose. I want a firm cause of death and a standard postmortem. Find out whatever you can about the guy."

"I'm at Mount Sinai right now, attending a lecture on environmental factors and skeletal decomposition," Levine said. She hesitated a moment. "That's Mount Sinai Hospital in Manhattan, not Mount Sinai on the Sinai Peninsula."

"Thanks for clarifying," Erin said in a level tone. "When can you make it down to Bellevue?"

"Approximately two hours, with a variance of twelve minutes depending on taxi availability and traffic lights."

"Okay, thanks. I'll let them know you're coming."

Erin hung up and saw Nelson watching her. "What?" she asked.

"You guys have that crazy lady Medical Examiner down there at the Eightball, don't you?" he said. "I've heard about her."

"She can be a little weird," Erin admitted. "But she's not crazy. And she's as good as they come."

"Can I go sleep now?" Tammy slurred.

"Pretty soon," the EMT said. He looked at the police officers. "It's okay to move her. Just make sure she stays conscious. I think maybe she had a hit of fentanyl, not heroin."

Erin and Nelson winced. Fentanyl was a synthetic opioid that could pack a punch a hundred times stronger than heroin. It was a common source of accidental overdoses, even among experienced drug users.

"That explains him," Nelson said, tilting his head toward the Mercedes. "I bet the two of them were out partying, got some of the good stuff, and it was better than they expected. Boom, dead. Open and shut. Hey, maybe I could be a detective."

"Maybe," Erin said. But Webb was right. It wasn't fair, but it was the way the world worked. Some deaths got more attention than others. She wasn't going to make any assumptions on this one.

Chapter 3

The 19th Precinct station was a classy building, in better condition than Erin's Precinct 8; concrete on the ground floor and red brick upper stories. Erin accompanied Tammy in the front. The girl wasn't under arrest; a funny quirk of drug laws didn't allow you to get busted for possession if the drug was already in your system. Erin wondered about that. Having a narcotic in your bloodstream definitely indicated possessing it to her, and it provided a risky way to avoid getting caught with drugs on your person, but that was a question for the lawyers. The NYPD could, however, hold her until she was sober.

Tammy didn't seem to mind. She sat in the drunk tank drawing on the wall with a fingertip, a dreamy look on her face. Erin wasn't sure the girl even realized she was in a police station. There was nothing to do but wait for her to come back to Earth.

While she waited, Erin helped Sergeant Nelson fill out one of the NYPD's ubiquitous DD-5 forms. Every cop knew the DD-5. As the departmental catchphrase said, "If it's not on a Five, it didn't happen." They were the foundation of the skyscraper that was police paperwork. It wasn't what Erin wanted to do with her day off.

After an hour, she went back to check on Tammy again. As she approached the holding cell, Erin paused. She heard what sounded like crying.

Sure enough, Tammy was bent double, her head in her hands, sobbing quietly. Apparently, she'd sobered up enough to remember at least some of what had happened.

Erin cleared her throat. "Tammy?"

Tammy looked up through her fingers. The tears had finished the destruction of her makeup. She was an absolute mess of badly-applied runny mascara and lipstick. Erin reflected that the more you put on, the worse you looked when things went wrong.

"How are you feeling?" Erin asked.

"Sick. Like I'm going to throw up."

Erin pointed to the stainless-steel toilet. Tammy looked at it, then back at Erin.

"Where am I?" the girl asked.

"Police station. The One Nine, in Manhattan."

"Who are you?"

"My name's Erin O'Reilly. I'm the detective who met you outside. What's your name?"

"Tammy... Tamara Cartwright."

"How old are you, Tammy?"

"Six..." she hiccupped. "Sixteen."

Erin flinched inwardly. Just a kid. That didn't really affect the situation. Tammy was a witness and a person of interest in a death. She didn't need parental consent to talk to the girl.

"Do you remember how you got here, Tammy?" she asked.

Tammy shook her head.

"What's the last thing you do remember?" Erin asked.

"I was in a dark room," Tammy said quietly. "With red lights. Like flames. It was loud. Lots of people."

"Were you with anyone?"

Tammy nodded. "My friends Paige and Hailey."

"Are they your age? The same year in school?"

Tammy nodded again.

"This dark room," Erin said. "Was it some sort of club?"

"I think so," Tammy said.

"You've got to be twenty-one to get into a Manhattan club," Erin said.

Tammy said nothing.

"Did you have a fake ID?" Erin asked.

Tammy continued to say nothing.

Erin sighed. "Look, Tammy, I'm with Major Crimes. I don't care if you were underage and sneaking into a club. I care about what happened to Martin Ross."

"Who?"

"The young man you were with. In the car."

"Oh, right. The car." Tammy shuddered and clutched at herself. She looked down at her arms and legs, as if seeing them for the first time. "Where are my clothes?"

Erin was puzzled. "You're wearing them."

"No, these aren't mine."

"That's what you had on when I met you," Erin said, inwardly adding, *looking like a cheap hooker on a Friday night.*

"They're not mine," Tammy repeated. "Mom would kill me if she saw me dressed like this. What time is it?"

"Going on one-thirty."

"In the morning?"

Erin smiled. "No, afternoon."

"Oh, no," Tammy said. "Mom *is* going to kill me. I was supposed to be home by midnight."

"You were walking down Madison Avenue in broad daylight," Erin said. "Is this the first time you've used fentanyl?"

"What's that?"

"Fentanyl," Erin repeated. "Synthetic heroin?"

Tammy's mouth fell open. "I didn't... I don't... I never..." she stammered.

"Tammy," Erin said. "I need you to tell me everything you remember. You were in the club. What happened next?"

"I remember a black man with red eyes," Tammy said. "I think I got a drink from him."

"Was he a guy at the club?" Erin asked.

Tammy screwed up her face, concentrating. She flinched and put a hand to her head. "I think he was selling drinks," she said.

"The bartender?"

"I think so. I hadn't had liquor before. Just that one time Paige snuck her dad's whiskey after the pep rally. I think maybe I got drunk."

"What happened next?" Erin asked.

"I don't know," Tammy said. "I remember talking to another guy at the bar."

"What did this other guy look like?"

"Older. Like my dad. Gray hair, wearing a suit. He was really into me."

"I'll bet," Erin said grimly. "Then what?"

"I got a little fuzzy. Maybe I fell asleep? The next thing I remember is the car. I was in the back seat of a car, I think, and there was this other guy."

"The same guy who was talking to you at the bar?"

"No. Younger." Tammy made a face. "He had his pants down."

"Did he do anything to you?" Erin asked.

"Like what?" Tammy asked. Then she made another face. "Eww, no. Except..." She shifted and a look of intense mortification came into her face. "Oh, no."

"What?" Erin asked, leaning forward against the bars of the cell.

Tammy glanced around, making sure no one else could hear them. "I'm not wearing any... you know..."

"Underwear?" Erin guessed.

Tammy nodded.

"Do you think you've been assaulted, Tammy?" Erin asked. "If you were drugged, you might not remember it. Do you have any pain or discomfort?"

Tammy shook her head. "I... I don't think so... God, what happened to me?" New tears filled her eyes. "I want to go home."

"We'll get you home as soon as we can," Erin promised. "This young man in the car. Did you recognize him? Had you seen him before?"

Tammy's head kept moving from side to side. "No," she sniffled. "Was he trying to... to... you know..."

"I don't know what he was doing, Tammy. Was he awake when you saw him?"

"No. He was just lying there. And he'd puked all over his shirt. It was really gross. It smelled really bad in the car, so I opened the door and got out, but I could barely walk. I fell over. I don't remember anything else."

"What was the name of the club?" Erin asked. "The one with the guy with the red eyes?"

"I don't remember."

"What are Paige and Hailey's last names?"

Tammy's eyes shifted. "I don't want to narc on them," she said.

Erin sighed again. "Tammy, the guy in the car is dead."

"Dead?" Tammy sucked in a breath. Then she nodded. "I thought so. I thought maybe he was just sick, but maybe I knew it." A tear rolled down her cheek. "I know I was supposed to be scared, but it was like I was all wrapped up in cotton balls. I couldn't feel anything, not really. You're not going to tell my mom, are you?"

"You're a minor, Tammy. I have to call your parents. They'll come get you."

"They're going to *kill* me," she said.

"No, they're not. They're going to be glad you're safe. They're probably really worried about you right now. If you had a midnight curfew, they'll be frantic."

"I'm going to be grounded *forever*."

Erin couldn't disagree with that assessment. "But they'll still be glad you're okay," she said. "My dad would've been pretty pissed if I'd had this happen to me, but he wouldn't have stopped loving me. It's going to be all right. Now, what's your phone number?"

Between sniffles, Tammy gave the number. Erin made the call.

The first ring hadn't even finished when the phone was snatched up on the other end. "Tammy?" a woman asked in a breathless, half-panicky voice.

"Mrs. Cartwright?" Erin guessed.

There was a pause. "Who is this?" the woman on the line asked.

"My name's Erin O'Reilly. I'm a detective with the NYPD. Your daughter—"

"Where is she?" Mrs. Cartwright interrupted. "What happened?"

"I'm right here with her, ma'am," Erin said. "Your daughter's going to be fine."

"Oh, thank God," the woman said. "I knew she was out somewhere with that Paige Brownlow, but Paige wouldn't give me a straight answer. Can I talk to her?"

"In a moment, ma'am," Erin said. "She's had a bit of a shock."

"Where are you?"

"We're at the 19th Precinct in Manhattan. I need to ask you a few questions, ma'am. Does your daughter know a man named Martin Ross?"

"Martin Ross? No, I don't think so," Mrs. Cartwright said. "But the name sounds familiar. I know it from somewhere. Maybe he's a boy at school with her?"

Erin let that drop. "You said she was out with Paige Brownlow. There may have been another girl with them, a Hailey. Do you know her?"

"Hailey Eversman," Mrs. Cartwright said at once. "They've been friends ever since preschool."

"Do you have contact information for Paige and Hailey?"

"Of course. I know their mothers."

"I'm going to need their telephone numbers," Erin said.

"If I give you that, will you please let me talk to my daughter?" Mrs. Cartwright said.

"Yes."

The woman gave Erin the information. Lacking her notebook, Erin jotted the numbers down on the back of her hand. Then she motioned Tammy over and handed her the phone.

"Mom?" Tammy said hesitantly.

Erin couldn't hear everything Tammy's mother said, but from what she could pick up, it sounded like a mixture of relief and anger. That was pretty much what she'd expected. Tammy did most of the listening and her mom did most of the talking.

While that conversation unfolded, a man came into the holding area. He was a tough-looking guy who somehow managed to wear a necktie while having essentially no neck to hang it on. He had a gold shield and a Glock 19 on his belt.

"You O'Reilly?" he asked by way of greeting.

"Erin O'Reilly, Major Crimes," she confirmed.

He offered his hand. "Lacroix, Manhattan Homicide. You working the Ross case?"

"Looks like it," she said, shaking with him. "There's something funny going on."

"Funny how?" He glanced at Tammy.

"There's a drug angle," she said. "And a group of underage girls. I don't have any answers yet."

"They took the victim to Bellevue, I heard," Lacroix said.

"Yeah," Erin said. "I'm going there next."

"Mind if I tag along?"

"What for? It's not a homicide." Erin paused. "Yet," she amended.

Lacroix shrugged. "My captain's worried about this case. It's political. I promise, I'll stay out of the way."

"Suit yourself," Erin said. "But I rode here with a Patrol guy."

"You don't have a car?" Lacroix asked, surprised.

"It's my day off," she said.

He laughed. "I'd hate to see you when you're working. You got what you need from her?"

"Everything except my phone," Erin said. "We just need to make sure we get her statement before she goes home."

Tammy hung up. Erin unlocked the holding cell and held out a hand. The girl dropped the phone into it.

"Is your mom coming to get you?" Erin asked.

Tammy nodded. "She's pissed, like you said, but she wasn't as mad as I thought."

"That's good," Erin said. "We'll need you to sign a statement. We can take care of that while we wait for her."

*   *   *

Ever since getting her gold shield, Erin had been spending a lot more time than she wanted in morgues. She hated the chemical smells that never quite managed to cover the familiar, unpleasant scent of blood and death. The furnishings, all stainless steel and tile, were cold, antiseptic, and impersonal.

It was no wonder Medical Examiners tended to be a little odd, working in a place like that, and Sarah Levine was a textbook example. Erin and Lacroix found her in the Bellevue Hospital morgue, clad in her ubiquitous lab coat and gloves, bent over the body of Martin Ross.

"What've you got, Doc?" Erin asked.

"Dead body," Levine said without looking up. "Male, early twenties. Temperature places time of death between midnight and one o' clock this morning."

"Overdose?" Erin guessed.

"I won't know until I run the bloodwork," Levine said.

"About that," Lacroix said. "There won't be any bloodwork."

Erin stared at him. "What did you say?"

He shrugged his massive shoulders slightly. "Sorry, O'Reilly. I got my orders. I'll be taking custody of Mr. Ross's remains now."

"On what authority?" Erin snapped. Her paranoia, never far from the surface these days, had jumped up like a jack-in-the-box.

"New York State Legislature," Lacroix said, producing a document with an official seal from inside his jacket. "Senator Ross has requested his son not be autopsied."

"He got the word fast," Erin observed. "Sounds like someone in the Department leaked the information."

"That's beside the point," Lacroix said. "Doesn't matter how he heard about it. I got the order right here if you want to read it."

Erin didn't touch the paper. "If you're really a detective, Lacroix, you know perfectly well that family members can't stop an autopsy if a death is suspicious."

"This isn't a family request," Lacroix said. "This is an official statement from the New York Senate. This is a national-security matter."

"National security?" Erin echoed incredulously. "We found him with his pants down and a drugged-up underage girl! You're going to tell me that's not a police matter?"

He shrugged again. "You got a problem, take it through channels. In the meantime, I'm taking the body."

"And breaking chain of evidence? Not a chance." Erin positioned herself between Lacroix and the slab on which Martin Ross's remains rested.

Lacroix shifted his stance ever so slightly, rising up on the balls of his feet and loosening his shoulders. "You don't want to do this, O'Reilly."

"Or what? You'll assault another officer?" Erin was angry now, but she was trying to keep her head clear. If Lacroix was confident enough of his position to risk threatening a fellow cop, he had serious political clout behind him. She wasn't afraid of him personally. He was a few inches taller than she was, and looked a lot stronger, but she'd faced down much scarier guys at close quarters. But she really wished she had Rolf with her.

Lacroix took a step forward. "I'm taking Ross, O'Reilly, and I'm walking out of here."

Erin took a quick look around the morgue. It was a lousy place for a fistfight, all hard surfaces and sharp corners. It would be like getting in a wrestling match in a bathroom. Broken bones and head injuries would be the likely result.

"Don't jostle me," Levine said abruptly. She straightened up from Ross's body. The Medical Examiner was holding a syringe in one hand.

"You don't want a part of this, get out of the way," Lacroix said.

"I'm holding thirty ccs of embalming fluid," Levine said. "If it's injected into a living body's bloodstream, it causes red blood cells to rupture and causes acidosis due to formic acid byproducts. The main effects of acidosis are organ dysfunction and death."

"Is that a threat?" Lacroix asked. It was his turn to be incredulous.

"It's a scientific statement of a predictable outcome," Levine said.

"You're not cutting him open," Lacroix said.

"Not at the moment," Levine said placidly. "The Y-incision will happen at a later stage in the autopsy."

Lacroix hesitated, but his stance became slightly less aggressive. Erin didn't relax. She didn't know this guy. He might try anything. Maybe he wasn't even a real cop. She hadn't run his credentials.

"How many enemies you got, O'Reilly?" he asked in a softer tone.

"Plenty," she said. "Most of them are in prison. Some are dead."

"Can you really afford another?"

"I'll take my chances," she said.

"I'm not talking about me," Lacroix said. "I'm nobody. I'm talking about Marcus Ross. You get on a state Senator's shit list, all kinds of misery rains down on you. I'm telling you, you want to walk away from this one."

"Thanks for the advice," Erin said. "I'll put it somewhere nice and safe, where the sun doesn't shine."

"Why don't you call your commanding officer?" Lacroix suggested. "Or better yet, your Captain? If you won't listen to me, maybe you'll listen to them."

"Back in grade school, when I ran into a playground bully, I didn't go running to the teacher."

Lacroix smiled slightly. "Tell you what, O'Reilly. Why don't we bring the temperature down a bit? Put Ross here on ice. He'll keep for a day or two, or a few hours at least. Hold off on the autopsy. We'll let the grownups sort out the red tape, and maybe we both walk off the playground with all our teeth."

"How's that sound to you, Doctor?" Erin asked without taking her eyes off Lacroix.

"Assuming proper preservation, I can delay the autopsy several days without ill effects," Levine said. She seemed a little confused. "Don't you usually want the results as quickly as possible? That's what you always say."

"This is a special case," Erin said.

"But you told me to come here as soon as I could," Levine said. "I walked out on my conference."

"And now I'm telling you to put him on ice," she said. "Secure the body, and I mean secure. No one's taking it, no one's touching it until we've cleared up the politics."

"Some specialized tests may be affected by a delay," Levine went on. "If cause of death was due to a chemical agent which breaks down over time, I may not be able to isolate the specific substance. However, the most likely causes will not be materially impacted."

"Is she always like this?" Lacroix asked, raising an eyebrow.

"What's it to you?" Erin shot back.

"Nothing personal, O'Reilly," he said. "I'm sure you're good police. We're all on the same team here."

"You sure about that?" she asked. "Because I'm working for the NYPD."

"So am I. And the people of New York State."

Erin nodded, but she wasn't convinced. She knew three things for sure. One was that she wasn't leaving Martin Ross's body unattended. Another thing was that she was going to find out about Detective Lacroix as soon as she had access to a computer. And third, he might be an asshole, but he was right. She needed to talk to Lieutenant Webb right away.

Lacroix had convinced her this was bigger than she'd thought. It wasn't just a matter of an accidental drug overdose. But what the hell was going on?

Erin didn't know, but she intended to find out.

Chapter 4

"You really stepped in it, O'Reilly."

Lieutenant Webb, hands on his hips, shook his head sadly. Vic Neshenko, standing just behind him, tried not to look smug and failed. They were in the hallway outside the hospital morgue. The other detectives had just arrived in answer to Erin's call. Lacroix had temporarily retreated upstairs. Levine was putting the finishing touches on Martin Ross's preservation.

"I didn't ask for any of this, sir," Erin said.

"Any trouble in the five boroughs, it always comes back to the Irish," Webb said.

"That's not fair, sir," she said. "The Italians cause their share."

"And the Russians," Vic added, grinning.

"I got a call from the Captain on the way over," Webb said. "He got a call from the Commissioner, who got a call from Senator Ross."

"Shit rolls downhill," Vic said, still grinning.

"You're enjoying this," Erin said.

"A little."

"There's plenty of shit," she said. "You'll get some on you before this is over, bet on it."

"That's fine," he said. "After a while, you don't even smell it anymore."

"They say the same thing about the morgue," she said. "It's not true."

"As I was saying," Webb said. "Senator Ross is very upset about the death of his son. Obviously."

"Doing all we can, swift justice, et cetera?" Vic guessed.

"No," Webb said. "Apparently, the honorable Marcus Ross, in his vast wisdom and experience as a legislator, has no need of the analytic skills honed by New York's Finest over its tenure as the oldest police force in the United States. He has already determined his son's death to be an unfortunate accident and has no wish for the matter to be further explored."

"Too bad that's not up to him," Erin said.

"You may find that it is," Webb said. "Senator Ross wields considerable power in New York."

"Like that asshole earlier this month with his Boston political connections?" Erin shot back. "He's in jail right now, because we put him there. What if Marcus Ross gave his son the drugs, and that's why he doesn't want us looking into it?"

"Be careful, O'Reilly," Webb said. "Especially when it comes to slinging accusations. I'd suggest thinking of Senator Ross the same way you would a powerful underworld boss. He's dangerous."

"Careful yourself, sir," Vic said. "She's living with one of those, didn't you hear? You're gonna get her all excited."

Erin gave Vic a dirty look. "You mean that, sir?" she asked Webb. "Is Ross going to try to have people killed?"

"I don't think he'd go quite that far," Webb said. "But he can kill your career. Give it to me straight, O'Reilly. Have you seen anything that suggests this was anything but an accidental overdose?"

"The girl," Erin said at once. "Tammy Cartwright."

"What about her?"

"I think she was abducted."

"By Martin Ross?" Webb asked sharply.

Erin shrugged. "She remembers talking to an older guy in a club. That guy might've been a procurer. Tammy's underage. If she was drugged and kidnapped, I don't want to walk away from this one."

"None of us do," Webb said, scowling. He had two teenage daughters from his first marriage. "But we have to watch our step. We've already seen the sort of wrench Ross can throw into our investigation."

"I recognized Lacroix when I got here," Vic said.

"Yeah?" Erin said with interest. "So he is a real cop? I was wondering."

"He's legit," Vic said. "A serious tough guy. We were in ESU together."

"Is he on the take?" she asked.

"How the hell would I know?" he retorted. "I haven't seen him in a couple years, not since he transferred to Homicide. And we were never close. But he's a bad guy to get on the wrong side of. I saw him throw a guy through a window once, during a bust."

"What floor of the building were you on?" Webb asked.

"Ground floor."

"That doesn't sound so bad," Erin said.

"The window was closed at the time," Vic said. "Tempered glass."

Erin and Webb both winced.

"Broke the guy's nose and both cheekbones," Vic went on. "Basically flattened his face. I heard the perp looked like a mummy at his indictment on account of all the bandages."

Erin was suddenly glad she hadn't mixed it up with Lacroix, at least without her K-9. "I want to look into him," she said.

"Only if it's pertinent to the case," Webb said. "First things first. We need to find out what happened."

"That's gonna be tricky if we can't touch the corpse," Vic said.

Webb opened the door to the morgue. "Doctor, can you come out here for a moment?" he called in.

Levine emerged. "What is it?" she asked with badly-disguised irritation.

"How's our victim?" Webb asked.

"Deceased."

Vic snorted.

"I meant, how is the preservation process coming along?" Webb rephrased.

"Done. Can I go now?"

"What can you tell us about cause of death?" he asked.

"Without doing bloodwork, it's only an educated guess," Levine said. "The most likely cause is opioid overdose, probably heroin or fentanyl."

"But if you had a blood sample," Erin said, "you could say for sure."

"We can't do anything else to the body," Webb said. "Not now that One PP is involved." He was talking about the Commissioner's office.

Erin nodded. "But suppose you'd come across a blood sample already," she said. "Before Lacroix and I arrived?"

"Could've come from anyone," Vic said. "Could've just been lying around in the morgue."

"That's not how chain of evidence works," Webb said, but he smiled slightly.

"It wouldn't be admissible in court," Erin said. "But it would give us some answers."

"Careful of poisoned fruit," Webb said.

The three detectives thought about this for a moment. Webb was referring to the doctrine of "fruit of the poisonous tree," a legal term which excluded not only illicitly-obtained evidence, but also anything found by use of that evidence. That could wreck any case they made.

"In your considered opinion," Erin said to Levine, "your best guess is he died of opioid use?"

"I just said that," Levine said impatiently.

"That's good enough for me," Erin said. "The EMT diagnosed Tammy with the same condition, the only difference being she was still alive. And he may have kept a blood sample from her. So I think we should operate on the assumption this is a drug-related case of negligent homicide."

"Sounds good to me," Vic said. "But we won't be able to trace the drugs unless we know whether the kid bought them, or someone gave them to him."

"He didn't have needle tracks," Levine said. "I hadn't proceeded to the main autopsy, but my external examination showed no signs of habitual narcotic usage. He had one needle mark just above the elbow on his right arm."

"Not a junkie," Webb said thoughtfully.

"There's a first time for everything," Vic said. "If he wasn't used to the stuff, no wonder he screwed up the dosage."

"No needles," Erin said suddenly.

"I'm sure that made sense in your head," Vic said. "But I'm not in there with you, thank God. Care to share?"

"In the car," she said. "Ross's Mercedes. I didn't see any drug paraphernalia. When did they shoot up? At the club, maybe?"

"Which club?" Webb asked.

She sighed. "I don't know. Tammy didn't remember."

"That's a good starting point," Webb said. "Try to find out where this girl was last night. If we can trace her movements, maybe we can work out whether she was snatched. But do it discreetly. Don't make waves. The two of you are on your own for this."

"Where'll you be, sir?" Vic asked.

"Giving you cover and camouflage," he said. "I'll be playing politics with the big boys."

"Do you want to be involved, sir?" Erin asked.

"I'm not," Webb said blandly. "I have no idea what you're talking about."

"What about you?" she asked Vic. "You want to risk your career by pissing off a politician?"

"Hell," he said. "I'll piss off a politician for *fun*. This is just gravy. Of course I'm in."

"Can I hitch a ride with you?" Erin asked. "I don't have my car, and I'm damned if I'm riding with Lacroix again."

"Sure," he said. "We gonna hit the club circuit?"

"That's the idea," she said. "But we need to make a stop first."

"What for?"

"I want to pick up Rolf."

"Great," Vic muttered. "He's gonna shed all over my backseat."

"My car's at my in-laws,'" she said. "You don't have to put up with Rolf. But for the record, he's the best-behaved member of Major Crimes."

"That," Webb said, "is a low bar to clear."

* * *

"Do you have any idea how many nightclubs there are in Manhattan?" Vic asked. He gave the wheel of his unmarked Taurus a savage twist and darted between a pair of taxis, drawing a honk from the one in back.

"Two or three," Erin said. "Eyes on the road."

"If I wasn't watching the road, could I do this?" he retorted, skating through the very tail end of a yellow light and easing past a double-parked van with only a breath and a coat of paint to spare.

Erin realized she'd clutched the dashboard in anticipation of a crash and made herself let go. "Next time I'm driving," she said.

"Why's that? Am I too much driver for you?"

"I don't want to die of testosterone poisoning," she replied.

Vic snickered. "Where am I driving, anyway?" he asked, easing back on the pedals slightly.

Erin brought up an address on the car's computer. "Tribeca," she said.

"There's no good clubs in Tribeca," Vic objected.

"We're not going to a club. We need to narrow the search. We're going to the Eversman residence."

"Who the hell are the Eversmans? Or is that Eversmen?"

"The daughter's a friend of Tammy's. According to her, they were out together last night."

"Good thing it's a Saturday," Vic said. "I'm sure she's just sitting at home, doing nothing, waiting for the five-oh to come knocking on her door."

"Have you ever tried not being sarcastic? I'm just wondering how your voice would sound."

"Tell you what. Because you're my partner, and we've been through all sorts of shit together, I promise never to be sarcastic with you again, for any reason, ever. Cross my heart, word of honor."

"You sound exactly the same."

"Gee, I wonder why."

"These girls were out drinking and partying last night," Erin said. "They're sixteen. Think back, Vic. If you were sixteen and you'd had a crazy night, when would you get out of bed?"

"When my mom dragged the sheets off me and opened the blinds," he said. "If then. You got a point. Maybe she's still asleep."

"Or nursing a hangover," she said. "Either way, her house is a good place to start."

"You want your dog first?"

"Hell yes. And I want my car. I wasn't kidding, the way you drive, you're going to die behind the wheel one of these days. And if I'm with you, I'm going down too. No thanks."

* * *

Michelle was full of questions when Erin showed up on the doorstep of the O'Reilly brownstone in Midtown. Erin hurriedly explained that she was on important police business while she put the leash on her K-9.

Rolf greeted Erin with a vigorously wagging tail and perked ears. The German Shepherd strongly suspected his partner had been working without him, which was against the rules, but he was willing to forgive her on the condition she took him along now.

Anna came down the stairs and stopped short when she saw Vic.

"Hi," she said.

"Hi," he replied.

"What happened to your nose?" she asked with nine-year-old directness.

"I broke a guy's hand with it," he said. Vic's nose had been bent well out of shape on more than one occasion, leaving him with a particularly rough-looking face.

"That looks like it hurt," she said.

"It did. He was in a cast for a month."

Anna giggled. "You're funny. Do you work with Auntie Erin?"

"Someone's got to get her out of trouble," Vic said.

"Sorry to run out on you, kiddo," Erin said.

"Are you going to catch the bad guy who killed that man in the car?" Anna asked.

"If we can," Erin said. "That's why I need Rolf. In case I need to chase him."

"Can you run faster than Rolfie?" Anna asked Vic.

"Never tried," Vic said.

"I can run faster than him," she declared.

Vic and Erin glanced at one another with raised eyebrows.

"Maybe he lets me win," Anna said after a moment's consideration.

"You're still invited to dinner," Michelle reminded Erin. Then she added, pointedly, "That's two invites."

"We'll see," Erin said noncommittally.

Out on the front steps, Vic said, "I don't suppose she meant me."

"No," Erin said.

"Carlyle?"

"Yeah."

"How'd that go over? With your dad and all?"

"Like none of your business."

*   *   *

Tribeca was one of the most expensive Manhattan neighborhoods. The Eversman residence was on the third floor of a corner apartment. Vic parked in the police spot right in front. Erin found a spot for her Charger a little further up the block. They met up on the sidewalk.

"How do you wanna play this?" Vic asked. "Good cop, bad cop?"

"I'll start as good cop," Erin said. "You can be bad cop."

"I'm always bad cop."

"You're good at it. And you like it, admit it."

"Yeah, I suppose. Let's go scare the hell out of a high school girl. God, that sounds creepy when I say it out loud."

Erin buzzed the Eversman apartment from the vestibule.

"Who is it?" a woman asked over the intercom.

"New York Police Department, ma'am," Erin said. "Can we come in?"

"Police? What's going on?"

"I'd like to discuss that in person."

"Oh, yes. I suppose. Yes, come in."

The lock on the lobby door disengaged with a heavy metallic sound. Vic glanced at it with professional interest on the way in.

"Good lock," he said. "Too good. Any crook worth his salt would just kick in the plate glass next to it."

The woman from the intercom was waiting at her apartment door. She was a lady of about forty, taking advantage of all the beauty-salon options available to an upper-class New Yorker. Her hair looked like it belonged on a billboard ad, her complexion was fantastic, and Erin would have bet her body had some post-factory improvements installed.

"Mrs. Eversman?" Erin asked.

"Connie," she said. "Officers?"

Hearing the tone of doubt in her voice when she saw Vic and Rolf, Erin produced her shield. "My name's Erin O'Reilly. This is Vic Neshenko. We're detectives with Major Crimes. Are you Hailey's mother?"

Connie's smile, which had faltered at the sight of Vic's scarred face, dropped away altogether. "Yes. What's this about?"

"Hailey's not in any trouble, ma'am," Erin said. "But we need to talk to her about one of her friends."

Connie's hand went to her mouth. "Oh my God. It's Tammy, isn't it? Tammy Cartwright? Did something happen to her?"

"What makes you say that?" Erin asked, always on the lookout for extra insights. Clues turned up in unlikely places.

"Deb Cartwright called me this morning, half out of her mind. Tammy never came home last night and she was hoping the girls had come back here together. I told her what Hailey told me."

"What was that?" Erin asked.

Connie looked up and down the hallway. Then she backed into her apartment and beckoned them to follow. She didn't say anything else until the door was closed behind the detectives.

"Hailey was out with Tammy and Paige," Connie said.

"Paige Brownlow?" Erin asked.

The other woman nodded. "They were going to an outdoor concert in Central Park. I wasn't sure about letting them go, but Dan said—"

"Dan?" Erin prompted gently.

"My husband. He said she'd only be young once, and some of his best memories were from going to concerts with his friends when he was her age." Connie shook her head. "If you want your kids to trust you, they say you should trust them. But Hailey came home and she was... Well, I don't want her to get in any trouble. I'd prefer to handle her discipline myself."

"We know about the drinking," Erin said. "Ma'am, we're Major Crimes detectives. We don't care if teenagers sneak a few beers. But we really do need to talk to Hailey. Would you mind seeing if she's awake?"

Mrs. Eversman retreated to her daughter's bedroom, leaving the detectives in the living room. Vic appraised the furnishings and nodded.

"I could get used to living in a place like this," he said. The room was tastefully decorated with quality furniture and artwork. The dining room had a chandelier that looked like real crystal.

"Not on a detective's salary," Erin said. Vic was living in a cluttered studio apartment and probably paying less than a quarter the rent the Eversmans were.

"Wonder what Dan does for a living," Vic said quietly. "Bet you ten bucks it's something shady."

"He's probably just a hedge fund manager or something," Erin said.

"Like I said, shady. Those Wall Street guys are all crooks."

Mrs. Eversman came back, trailed by her daughter. Hailey looked like a girl experiencing her first real hangover. The teenager would have been an unusually pretty blonde if she'd had the time and inclination to clean up, but at the moment her hair was a tangled rat's nest, her eyes were puffy, and she was squinting against the light.

"Hailey, these folks are from the police," Connie said. "They want to talk about Tammy."

Hailey blinked at them. Then she saw Rolf and her eyes went a little wider. Rolf's nostrils twitched and he cocked his head at her.

"I'm Erin O'Reilly," Erin said. "This is Detective Neshenko and Rolf, my K-9. We want to talk about what happened last night."

"Oh no," Hailey said. "Look, it was just the one, okay? I'd never done it before, and the guy was just passing it around, and I thought, what difference does it make? I was just being polite!"

"What guy was this?" Erin asked.

"The guy at the concert," Hailey said. "He said it was good stuff, and we should try it, and if we liked it there was more back at his place. I'm sorry! I didn't think!"

"You smoked a joint?" Vic guessed.

"I didn't know your dogs could still smell it the next day," she said.

"A good drug dog can," Erin said, leaving out the fact that Rolf wasn't trained in drug detection and had no idea marijuana was illegal. She remembered something her dad had told her about interrogations.

"Soldiers have an old saying that you shouldn't interrupt your enemy while he's making a mistake. Cops have one, too. Never interrupt your suspect in the middle of a confession. If you want to learn, you have to listen."

"Am I going to jail?" Hailey asked. She looked like she was about to cry.

"If you cooperate, and tell us the truth, we should be able to work things out right here," Erin said.

Connie was staring at her daughter in undisguised horror. "Hailey, you took *drugs* from a *stranger*?" she exclaimed. "There could have been *anything* in them!"

"Ma'am, please," Erin said. "You can discuss this with her later."

"Oh, we're going to discuss it," Connie said. Her mouth set in a thin line.

"You went to the concert," Erin said to Hailey, trying to get her back on track.

"Yeah," Hailey said. "With Paige and Tammy. It was the Earthman Experience, with DJ Hard Hittin' Henry."

Erin had no idea who that was, but she nodded as if she understood.

"The concert was at ten. I was supposed to be home by one, but I figured I could push that a little."

Connie's jaw tightened still further, but she said nothing.

"There were all kinds of people there," Hailey went on. "It was wild. And this guy came up to me and offered me... you know, the joint. I didn't know what to do. Paige said I should try it, that she'd been stoned before and it made the music better. So I thought, why not? I didn't like the smell, and it made me feel kinda funny. Tingly. The guy offered to go back to his place after the concert, and Paige thought it'd be fun, but I didn't think that was a real good idea. So she said I was a drag, but she knew a place we could go instead."

"Did anything else happen at the concert?" Erin asked.

"The music was cool," Hailey said. "And Paige made out with a guy."

"The guy who gave you the weed?"

"No, a different guy. And Tammy said the joint made her feel weird, too."

"So all three of you smoked?" Erin asked.

Hailey nodded. "We passed it around. Paige said there was something else in it, too. Not just weed."

Erin nodded again. Connie was right. Almost anything could be in a cigarette. "Wet" joints, ones that had been soaked in another substance, were the worst. Formaldehyde was popular. Smoking that could kill you.

"After the concert, we left the park," Hailey said. "Paige took us to this place where she knew the bouncer. We had our IDs, but they weren't really good. If you looked close, you could tell they were fake."

Connie Eversman looked like she was about fifteen seconds from strangling her daughter. Erin made a calming gesture with her hand and kept nodding and listening.

"So Paige talked to the guy at the door and he let us into the club," Hailey said.

"What was the name of this place?" Erin asked.

"Club Armageddon," Hailey said. "It was really dark inside, with these gas fireplace vents that would shoot out flames. Behind glass, of course, so you wouldn't get burned, but it was really warm in there. And crowded. I needed something to drink, because of the heat, you know. And my head still felt funny. So I had a couple of drinks."

Erin reflected that "a couple of drinks" was the most anyone ever admitted to drinking. It could mean anywhere from two to twenty.

"After a while, Paige had to go to the bathroom. She was pretty smashed, so I thought I should go with her. When we came out, Tammy wasn't there."

"Where did you see her last?" Erin asked.

"At the bar. She was talking to this guy."

"What did the guy look like?"

"Kind of like Dad. Going bald, wearing a suit. I don't know. It was dark, I didn't get a good look at him. But Paige was throwing up in the bathroom, so I was in there with her, holding her hair. It took a while, and when we came out, Tammy was gone. I figured she went home so she wouldn't get in trouble."

"What time was this?" Erin asked.

"Maybe one thirty," Hailey guessed. "We didn't have a clock and I'd turned off my phone."

"So I couldn't check up on her," Connie said grimly.

Hailey was definitely wide awake now, and Erin saw a thought hit her, suddenly and hard. The girl's face, already pale, went sheet white.

"You said you were detectives," Hailey said. "What kind?"

"Major Crimes," Vic said.

"You guys do, like, kidnapping and... and murder and stuff."

"That's right," Erin said gently.

"Is Tammy... okay?"

"She was lucky. She'll be all right. But it was a close shave. Here's my card. If you think of anything else, give me a call." Erin handed over a card.

Hailey took it, looking like her whole world had fallen apart. Judging from her mother's expression, that wasn't far short of the truth.

Chapter 5

"I'm never having kids," Vic announced once they were out on the pavement again.

"The human gene pool thanks you," Erin said.

"Seriously," he said. "Look where it gets you. We're living in a world where doing one stupid thing can get you killed. Those girls did five, six, hell, I don't even know how many. In a fair world, they'd all be on slabs at the morgue."

"If she'd gone back to that pot dealer's pad, there's a good chance she would've been raped," Erin said. "And Tammy was a whisker from a fatal overdose. But doing something risky doesn't mean you deserve whatever happens."

"I didn't mean that," Vic said. "Sorry."

"It's easy to blame victims," she pressed. "Lots of people do it. Especially guys, when a girl gets mistreated."

"Hey." Vic held up a hand. "Did I slap cuffs on our girl up there? Did I? Just 'cause you don't have a bad guy to beat up on doesn't mean you gotta take shots at me."

Erin sighed. "You're right. Sorry."

"I know I look like a chauvinist thug," Vic said. "That doesn't make me one."

"I said I was sorry. What do you want, a hug?"

Vic smiled. "No thanks, I'm good. What now? Club Armageddon?"

"Club Armageddon," she agreed.

*　　*　　*

The club was just a few blocks down Fifth Avenue from the Guggenheim, so Erin ended up almost exactly retracing her previous movements. It didn't look like much from the outside, just a basement entrance to a stone building. Erin, Vic, and Rolf assembled outside.

"Says they don't open until five," Vic said, examining the posted hours.

"Someone's probably here," Erin said. She knocked on the door, her fist banging dully on the sturdy-looking steel.

She had to knock twice more before a short man with spiky hair abruptly yanked the door open.

"We're closed," he snapped.

In answer, Erin held up her gold shield.

The man was already shoving the door shut, but Vic was quicker. He got his foot between the door and the frame. The door was solid metal and looked heavy, but to judge from Vic's face, he got his limbs smashed in doors all the time. He didn't flinch, didn't even blink.

"We're cops, buddy," Vic said. "And it's a good thing we're charitable cops, or we might be inclined to be suspicious, the way you slammed the door on us."

The little guy took a half-step back and held up his hands. "Whoa there. I didn't, you know, register. What's the problem?"

"We're looking for some information about a girl who was in here last night," Erin said.

"I don't know nothing about that. I wasn't here last night."

"Do you have a bartender who's got dark skin?" Erin asked. Then, feeling a little silly, she added, "And red eyes, maybe?"

Recognition sparked in the man's face. "You mean Marv?"

"If she knew his name, don't you think she'd have said it?" Vic asked.

"Smartass," the little guy muttered. "Marv's the only guy who looks like that around here."

"Is he here now?" Erin asked.

"Nah, he don't come on till we open. Works five to one."

"You have security cameras?"

"Course we do."

"Do they work?" Vic asked. Cops knew a lot of cameras were just there as deterrents. Half the time they weren't even turned on.

"What do you think?"

"I think I'd like you to answer the question," Vic growled.

"We need to see the footage from last night," Erin said.

"You got a warrant?"

"I can get one," Erin said.

"You go do that," he said. "Then come back here. In the meantime, stop blocking daylight."

He pushed on the door again. Vic left his foot there for a second, just to make the point that he'd move when he was good and ready. Then he retracted it. The door closed with a bang.

"I love dealing with the public," Vic said. "It helps me understand murderers better. Empathize, you know? You gonna get the warrant?"

"I was bluffing," she said. "We don't want to put in for any warrants yet. Webb said to keep this low-key, so I think we should stay off the record as much as possible."

Vic nodded. "So what do you wanna do?"

"I'll come back tonight, when they're open," she decided.

"Okay. You want backup?"

"You'll be coming off a full shift," she said. "Forget about it. I'll go to dinner at my brother's and then come out here. I'll be fine."

"You sure? It sounds like maybe a girl got snatched from here."

"Vic, I live over a mob bar, remember? I can take care of myself. And I'll have Rolf if things go sideways."

"Your funeral."

"So I think we'd better do some more digging on Martin Ross in the meantime," she said. "Find out his priors, see if he might've grabbed Tammy. And I'm wondering about the clothes."

"What clothes?"

"Tammy was dressed like a streetwalker. But she said the clothes weren't hers."

Vic laughed. "That's a new one. I bet Sergeant Brown in Vice never had a hooker tell him that."

"And her makeup was sloppy," Erin went on.

"Stop it, Erin."

"What?"

"You're sounding too much like a girl. Now it's clothes and makeup, next it'll be boy bands and vampire romance novels. I like you better when you're a hardass. And you do know it's still your day off, right?"

Erin smiled. "You're right. If I put in for overtime, I'll need to say why. And we don't want the paper trail. I guess I'll get out of your hair."

"I'll run a background on the Senator's kid," Vic promised. "I'll find something for sure. All these rich brats have skeletons in their closets."

"Quietly," she reminded him.

"Don't worry, I'll be real discreet. I'm like a ninja."

Erin gave him a dubious look. Rolf sat and scratched himself, managing to look both dismissive and skeptical.

"Whatever," Vic said. "Get outta here, and take that mangy mutt with you. I'll see you tomorrow."

"I'll be a little later coming in," she said.

"What for?"

"I'm going to Mass."

"Jesus Christ, why? You got some sins on your conscience?"

"I was planning on praying for you," she said, smiling sweetly. "You've got a lot to answer to the big guy for."

"Don't bother. I'm a lost cause."

"See you tomorrow, Vic."

*   *   *

"Welcome home, darling," Carlyle called down the hall. "How was the museum?"

"Surprising," Erin said. "Where are you?"

"In the study, going over the accounts."

Erin and Rolf went to meet him. They found him at his desk, his laptop open in front of him. He stood when she entered the room, as he always did. He rose to his full height with only a slight wince, which Erin noted. He'd bounced back well from the stomach wound he'd received at the beginning of the month. While he wasn't completely healed, he was in pretty good shape.

She gave him a quick kiss. Rolf gave Carlyle a businesslike sniff of the hand. The K-9 accepted the Irishman, since Erin obviously liked him, but Rolf was slow to completely trust.

"Surprises aren't often appreciated in your line of work," Carlyle observed. "Nor mine, come to that."

"It wasn't the museum. It was what happened outside."

He raised an eyebrow.

"Sit down," she suggested. "It's a long story."

"I hope it's nothing to do with our present situation," he said, resuming his seat.

"That depends. Are the O'Malleys associated with Senator Ross?"

"Marcus Ross? Nay, Evan's not as well-connected as all that. Is the Senator in some sort of trouble?"

"You could say that. It's about his son." She quickly explained what had happened, including the interference from Detective Lacroix.

Carlyle listened intently, his hands clasped on his desk. When she'd finished, he nodded thoughtfully.

"Even when you're away from work, there's no escaping it," he said with a faint smile.

"I'm a cop," she said. "This isn't just what I do, it's who I am."

"I'd not have it otherwise. Do you think the lad was murdered?"

"How can we possibly know? Without access to the body, it's going to be hard to rule the death a homicide, or a suicide, or an accident."

"Do you believe the lass was drugged against her will?"

Erin had been considering this. "I think so," she said. "The girls took some drugs at the concert. If the weed was spiked with something else, that might've been why Tammy blacked out. But that wouldn't explain Ross's death. We don't have any reason to believe he was at the concert. It'd be one hell of a coincidence for him to get the same bad batch of drugs independently."

"That's unlikely, I agree," he said. "Your examiner believes it was fentanyl?"

"Probably, but without bloodwork, we can't prove it."

"Your lot do get hung up on proof," Carlyle said, smiling. "Suspicion's quite enough for my lads to go on. I can't be much help with the Senator, but I may be able to assist in the matter of narcotics."

"I know the O'Malleys handle heroin," Erin said. "Veronica Blackburn's in charge of it now." Veronica had taken over from Evan O'Malley's previous drug boss, Liam McIntyre, after an unfortunate incident earlier in the year had left Liam with a few extra holes.

"And fentanyl," Carlyle agreed. "Among other things. But she's hardly the only one in New York. I assume you've access to the bloodwork from the lass, even if you've nothing from young Mr. Ross. I could, perhaps, provide you with a wee sample of the stuff from the O'Malley stores to provide a basis for testing."

Erin gave him a sharp look. "Is that safe? Everyone knows you don't use. It'll look suspicious if you start asking for dime bags."

"Erin, darling, give me a bit of credit for discretion. I'll work through one of my intermediaries. Give me a day and I'll have something for you. And if you're looking for competitors' merchandise, I'll wager I can lay my hands on a bit of that, too. I'll have Corky handle it. He'll enjoy the experience."

"Corky enjoys every experience," Erin said sourly. "But thanks, that'd be helpful. If we can identify the drug pipeline, it may help us figure out what happened."

"Grand," he said, smiling. "I'll also make inquiries about the Senator. If he'd any underworld dealings, someone will know."

"Okay," she said. "But be discreet. In this case, we don't want word leaking out to my people any more than to yours."

He nodded. "It's settled. Will you be dining here this evening? I know you were planning to sup with your relations, but that may have changed."

"No, I'm still invited to dinner with Junior and his family," she said. "So are you, now that you mention it."

"And your thoughts on the subject?"

Erin shrugged. "Michelle's been wanting to meet you for a while. I guess we have to, sooner or later. It'd be better to do it at her place. At least their house isn't full of..."

"Gangsters?"

"Yeah."

"I'd be delighted to accept their invitation," he said.

"Are you feeling up for it? Speaking of narcotics, are you taking your meds?"

"I swore off the Vicodin two days ago." He held up a hand, seeing her open her mouth to object. "Darling, a clear head's a necessity. The last thing I'm needing is to be going all foggy when I'm talking to Evan or, God help us, Mickey. I need to stay sharp. A bit of pain on top of the sobriety's a small price to pay. In fact, it helps me focus."

"If you're hurting, you should stay home. I'll tell Shelley you're still recuperating."

"Nonsense, darling, this is your family. I promise I'll not overexert myself."

Erin was doubtful, but she nodded. "Okay, if you insist."

* * *

Riding back to Midtown in Carlyle's Mercedes with Ian Thompson behind the wheel, Carlyle up front, and Rolf in the back beside her, Erin was nervous. This was the first encounter between her family and Carlyle in his capacity as her boyfriend. She reminded herself she wasn't a teenager anymore. Besides, this wasn't meeting the parents. This was her brother and his family. Michelle was a hopeless romantic and was already firmly in Erin's corner. There was nothing to worry about.

Erin worried all the way there.

Michelle's hostess radar must have locked onto their approach. Erin was offering a hand to help Carlyle out of the car when the brownstone's front door swung open. Ian, standing on the driver's side, hyper-alert as always, pivoted and dropped a hand inside his coat. Her saw the woman in the doorway and relaxed slightly, turning his attention back to the street.

"Welcome!" Michelle called. She came down the steps to the sidewalk. "You must be Erin's beau. I'm Shelley. I'm delighted to finally meet you!"

Carlyle smiled and extended a hand. "Morton Carlyle, at your service. Erin's told me so very much about you." He was wearing one of his best suits, a gray Armani with a fine silk necktie and matching pocket square. In his left hand he held a brown paper bag. He was every inch the smooth gentleman.

Michelle ignored his hand and kissed him on both cheeks instead. "Sis has been spreading gossip, has she? That's not quite fair. I've only heard rumors about you. Thank you so much for coming! I'm looking forward to filling in all the gaps. The food's almost ready. Come in, come in. Oh!"

She'd caught sight of Ian. The driver was still standing in the street, making sure the coast was clear. Erin wondered whether Ian really saw Manhattan, or if he still had one eye on Fallujah or Kandahar. The former Marine was never truly out of his personal combat zone.

"We have plenty for one more place at the table," she said. "Doesn't your man there want to come in?"

Carlyle glanced at Ian.

"I'm fine, ma'am," Ian said. "Thank you for asking."

"What's that supposed to mean?" Michelle retorted. "What are you going to eat? I'm making French duck confit with dressing. I promise, it's delicious."

Ian seemed a little embarrassed, which was a new expression on his face for Erin. She hid a smile.

"I'll bet it's better than anything they gave you in the Corps," Erin teased.

"I'm on duty, ma'am," he said.

"Can you do your duty from inside the house?" Michelle asked, putting her hands on her hips.

"I guess so, ma'am."

"Then you're coming in," she said in tones of finality.

That was how Erin, Carlyle, Rolf, and Ian ended up in the O'Reilly dining room with Michelle, Sean Junior, Patrick, and Anna. Erin noted Ian made sure to take a seat which gave him a good view of all the entrances to the room. He still seemed tense.

Sean shook hands with Carlyle. "It's nice to officially meet you," he said.

"I've been looking for the opportunity to thank you in person," Carlyle said. "I fear I was hardly at my best at our first meeting."

"I've seen worse," Sean said. "How's the stomach?" At their first meeting, Carlyle had been lying on a blood-soaked stretcher, clinging to life by his fingernails. Erin guessed most of the worse cases her brother had seen had ended in death.

"I'm certain it'll be grand once it's filled with what your charming wife's planning on supplying," Carlyle said. He produced an oblong box tied with a green ribbon from his bag. "Here's a wee something for the host and hostess."

"Ooh, let me see!" Michelle exclaimed. She opened the box to reveal a bottle of rich amber liquid, emblazoned with the name Glen Docherty-Kinlochewe.

"That's the good stuff," Erin said. It was her favorite brand of whiskey, from a distillery in the Scottish Highlands. She had an identical bottle in their liquor cabinet.

"What about for me?" Anna asked. "All I get to drink is juice boxes. Mom says I'm too young for whiskey."

"Anna, don't be greedy," Michelle said.

"Your mum's right," Carlyle said gravely. "You're a mite too young for the hard stuff. Now, what might I have for a fair wee lass?"

Wearing an expression of mock concern, he looked in his bag once more and came out with a smaller box, only an inch thick and about three inches on a side.

"Ah, here we are! What do you think of that?" he asked.

Anna eagerly opened the box and found a slender silver bracelet decorated with Celtic knotwork and a pair of molded hands holding a heart and crown.

"What's this?" Anna asked.

"That's a Claddagh bracelet, darling," he said. "The Claddagh is a very old Irish symbol. It stands for love, loyalty, and friendship."

Anna slipped the bracelet onto her wrist and sat happily, admiring it. "It's pretty," she said. "Thank you, Mr. Morton."

Carlyle laughed. "Now that's something no one's called me before. That only leaves one." He turned to Patrick, who looked up at him with curiosity and a sort of quiet hopefulness.

"And here it is," Carlyle said, his hand emerging with something white and fluffy. It was a plush sheep, Erin saw with amusement. Patrick, six years old, was definitely still of an age to like stuffed animals. When Carlyle handed it over, the boy took hold and immediately held it close.

"Not at the dinner table, dear," Michelle said. "It'll get food all over it. You can have it again after supper. All right, everyone, let's eat!"

Patrick sullenly surrendered the sheep and dinner proceeded.

The food was as tasty as always. Michelle vied with Erin's mom for the title of best cook in the family. Erin didn't think she'd ever eaten exactly the same meal at her brother's house. While she ate, she watched and listened.

Pretty much every gangster had done prison time. It was inevitable, one of the costs of doing business. Carlyle was the only exception Erin had ever encountered in the upper echelons of organized crime. He'd never even been arrested in the United States. But he'd faced his share of police inquiries, hard-nosed detectives who knew the right questions to ask and how to get answers. Even so, Erin doubted he'd ever met a more formidable interrogator than Michelle O'Reilly.

She started with the easy questions, the obvious ones like how he and Erin had met. That led her to his background, his life in Ireland prior to immigrating. He fielded those easily enough. None of them even required him to bend the truth. But then she mentioned how hard it must have been growing up in Belfast during the Troubles, and from then on, she was on him like Rolf on a bite sleeve.

"Were you involved with the IRA?" she asked.

"A Catholic lad was bound to come in contact with them at one point or another," Carlyle said, deftly sidestepping.

Michelle smelled the deception. "Did you serve with them?" she pressed.

"My da was in the Brigades," he said, deflecting again.

"Your father? What happened to him?"

"The Brits killed him during a raid."

"Oh no! I'm so sorry!"

For a moment, Erin thought Carlyle had successfully turned the subject, but a minute later, Michelle was back on it.

"So did you join up to get revenge?" Michelle asked.

"I never said I was a part of it myself," Carlyle said.

"And you never said you weren't."

"Darling, if it weren't for this lovely meal you've provided, I'd be a mite concerned about how you treat your visitors."

Sean put a hand on his wife's arm. "Shelley, give the man a break. Can't you see he doesn't like to talk about it?"

"His wife was killed in the Troubles, too," Erin added quietly.

Michelle was instantly contrite. "Oh, of course," she said. "I'm sorry. Forget I asked about it. I can be so thoughtless sometimes. So, what's it like running a bar?"

"It's a public house, not a bar," he said with a smile. "And it's a grand life. I think I'd not want to do anything else."

That diverted the conversation to the subject of pubs and the challenges of running a business in Manhattan. Carlyle didn't say anything about his Mob dealings, but with the surgeon who'd operated on him sitting at the table, there was one aspect of his other life that was bound to come up sooner or later.

It happened over dessert, which was white chocolate scones with a strawberry sauce. Sean was watching Carlyle eat with professional interest.

"Everything working all right?" the doctor asked.

"Aye, you did a grand job patching me up," Carlyle said. "A lad might think you'd some practice."

"Too much," Sean sighed. "You see a lot of GSWs in the ER. Not all deliberate shootings, either. You know how many kids I've had come in because they got their hands on one of Dad's guns?"

"Never assume malice when carelessness is sufficient explanation," Carlyle agreed. "The trouble with firearms is that they make it easy to kill without meaning to. If a lad stabs you with a knife, whatever you may have done, you can rest assured he meant to stick you."

"I'm interested in murders," Anna announced, to Michelle's intense mortification.

"Solving them, not committing them, I hope," Erin said.

"Of course," Anna said. "Like that man in the car today. I want to figure out what happened to him. I'm going to be a cop, just like Auntie Erin. I'll get a gold shield and everything."

"And you'll be a fine one, I've no doubt," Carlyle said.

"What about you, Ian?" Michelle asked.

"What about me, ma'am?" That was the longest thing he'd said the whole meal.

"What's your story?"

"Not much to tell, ma'am."

"You say 'ma'am' a lot," Anna observed. "Why?"

"They taught me to be polite," Ian said.

"Who's 'they?'" Anna asked.

"Marine Corps, Miss."

"You're a soldier?"

"Marine," he corrected gently.

"Are you a hero?"

Erin winced. That was one of the questions you never asked a combat veteran.

"I don't think so," Ian said. "How would I know?"

While Erin was wondering how to delicately intervene, Anna went ahead and asked the second big no-no.

"Did you ever shoot anyone?"

"Anna!" Michelle exclaimed, horrified.

Ian bent down so his head was almost on a level with the little girl's. "I did my job, Miss O'Reilly," he said quietly. "I did what I had to do."

Anna looked into his calm, neutral face for a moment, trying to figure out what he meant. Then she nodded.

"Was it scary?" she asked.

Ian's eyebrows drew together slightly. "What?"

"Being in the war. Were you scared?"

"Anna, you're not being polite," Michelle hissed.

"Mom says I ask too many questions," Anna said.

"Sometimes I got scared," Ian said. "War can be scary."

"Does war hurt?"

Ian reflexively flexed his shoulder. "They fixed me up pretty well."

"No, silly," Anna said. "I mean here." She reached out and laid a finger against Ian's shirt front, right over his heart.

Ian's jaw worked silently. Then, still without saying anything, he nodded once.

"I'm sorry," Anna said. Then she slid out of her chair and, before anyone could do anything, wrapped her arms around Ian and gave him a big hug.

The adults around the table exchanged glances. Michelle was a mix of shocked and embarrassed. Sean just looked surprised. Carlyle was thoughtful. And Erin smiled, because she was looking at Ian's face. She saw a softness she'd never seen in it before as he put his left arm around the little girl's shoulders and gave her a brief squeeze.

*   *   *

When a hostess asked a guest to help with the dishes, what she was really saying was that she wanted a private word away from the rest of the household. Carlyle and Ian went into the living room with Sean. Anna and Patrick started a game of hide and seek with Rolf, which Erin considered a sort of unofficial training for the K-9. And Erin ended up in the kitchen with her sister-in-law.

"Okay, Shelley," Erin said. "Hit me with it. What's your verdict?"

"I love him," Michelle said. "I absolutely love him. He's so polite, so pleasant, and that *accent!*"

"You can't have him," Erin said. "I saw him first."

"Oh, I know. But I can't believe you've kept him away all this time!"

"You know why."

"Oh, that," Michelle said, dismissing the whole organized-crime angle with a wave of her hand. "You'll figure something out. He can't possibly be a bad guy, or you wouldn't have fallen for him. But he does have his secrets. He was in the IRA, wasn't he?"

"Allegedly?" Erin asked with a smile.

"Will you stop being a cop for five minutes?"

"I can't. I don't know how."

Michelle pouted. "What did he do for them?"

"Do you really want to know?"

"No, Erin, I just asked to hear the sound of my own voice. Of course I want to know! Give me some secondhand adventures. They're the only kind I get. You know Anna's hardly stopped talking about the body in the car today? She thought it was exciting. I thought it was horrible, but she was right, too."

"He built car bombs," Erin said bluntly.

Michelle stared at her, looking for some sign of humor. "You're serious?"

"Yeah."

"My God. Did he ever... you know... did anyone..."

"Didn't you just tell your daughter not to ask rude questions?" Erin replied. She was getting good at Carlyle's style of conversation.

"But he doesn't do that anymore, does he?"

"No."

"And his driver, or whatever he is..."

"Ian?"

"He's something else."

"You have no idea," Erin said. "He's saved my life. Two, maybe three times."

"He's quiet, but very courteous. Good-looking, too. He takes care of himself and he's good with kids. I noticed he wasn't wearing a ring. I was just wondering..."

"You're a married woman, Shelley!"

"No! Not that! I was wondering why he hadn't settled down with someone."

"I don't think he knows how to settle down," Erin said. "He had some really bad experiences over there. I think he needs to make peace with himself before he could open up to someone else."

"He opened up to Anna a little," Michelle said.

"Yeah, I saw that," Erin said. "It surprised me. If that kid decides not to be a cop, maybe she's got a future as a therapist."

"Did you find out anything about the man in the car?" Michelle asked. Apparently, thinking of therapists got her mind on traumatic events.

"We're working on it," Erin said.

"Was he murdered?"

"That depends on intention."

"How can you tell intention?"

"We find the right guy and ask."

Chapter 6

"That went rather well, I thought," Carlyle said.

They were in his Mercedes, on their way back to the Barley Corner. Rolf had curled up into a furry ball next to Erin, with his snout tucked under his tail. Erin was rubbing his shoulder

"Yeah," Erin said. "But those aren't the O'Reillys you need to worry about."

"Your da will come round," Carlyle said. "It's just a matter of diplomacy."

"Family politics are the worst politics," she said darkly.

"I've heard that's why the Great War started," he replied. "All the crowned heads of Europe were cousins and whatnot, so a common family squabble wound up essentially destroying the continent."

"Why doesn't Senator Ross want us finding out what happened to his kid?" she wondered aloud. The subject of family politics had put her in mind of the dead young man and his powerful father.

"I can think of a few reasons," Carlyle said. "What about you, Ian?"

"Me?" Ian sounded surprised. "No opinion, sir."

"Speculate, please," Carlyle said.

"I guess I can think of two reasons a guy might not want you to know, sir," Ian said. "Either he already knows, or he doesn't want to know."

"You're right, lad," Carlyle said. "I've a third option. Perhaps the dear Senator isn't interested in official consequences. If someone hurt his lad, he may be interested in more personal retribution."

Erin hadn't thought of that. "That's a good point," she said. "From a gangster perspective."

"If you wanted a clergyman's take on this, you'd be talking to a priest," he said with a chuckle. "On that subject, will you be accompanying me to Mass in the morning?"

"That's the plan," she said. "You up for it?" It would be Carlyle's first trip to church since the shooting.

"It'll be good for me, I'm thinking," he said.

Erin wondered about that. Phil Stachowski, her undercover case officer, had told her it would help to have some sort of spiritual reinforcement. But while she'd been raised Catholic, and still considered herself to be, she didn't usually give religion much thought.

"You Catholic, Ian?" she asked.

"No, ma'am."

"What are you?"

"I'm a Marine, ma'am."

"I mean, what do you believe in?"

"This is my rifle," Ian said, with the tone of a man reciting something he knew by heart. "There are many like it, but this one is mine. My rifle is my best friend. It is my life. I must master it as I must master my life. My rifle, without me, is useless. Without my rifle, I am useless."

"You don't even carry a rifle these days," she reminded him.

"Got a couple back at my place," he said. "In case I need them."

"It's the principle of the thing," Carlyle said.

"You don't believe in God?" she asked Ian.

She saw his shrug over his seatback. "Don't think He cares much what I believe. Can't count on Him when the chips are down."

"When the chips are down, He's all you can count on," Carlyle said softly.

"Not in my experience, sir."

"Who do you think got you out of Afghanistan?" Carlyle countered.

"Walked most of the way," Ian said. "Army guys drove me the rest of it."

"And who sent the Army lads?"

"Their CO. They weren't looking for me. Just dumb luck they ran into me."

"I've heard it said that miracles mostly boil down to timing," Carlyle said. "If you hadn't been rescued in Afghanistan, you'd not have been there to rescue Erin and me in turn. Everything connects. In life, it comes down to who you know most of the time. And I'd like the Almighty to be in my corner, when all's done. There's no better networking than that."

"I wouldn't mind a gunship flying close air support," Ian said.

"You're more talkative than usual tonight," Erin commented.

"Sorry, ma'am. No excuse."

"Now that's more like the Ian I know," she said, smiling. "Anna likes you. Patrick, too, I think. But he's harder to read."

Ian kept staring straight ahead, watching the road. "I like kids," he said quietly.

"And they like you," she said.

"Not all of them," he said. And that was all she got out of Ian on that drive.

*   *   *

The Barley Corner was full to capacity when they got there. Erin knew Carlyle was tired. He'd enjoyed the visit with the O'Reillys, but now she could see the strain in the set of his jaw and the tightness around his eyes. She steered him toward the stairs, but it wasn't that simple. Being a mobster was in many ways like being a politician—a politician in a third-world warzone where rival warlords were always thinking about assassinations. Hard-faced men kept coming up to them and wanting to talk to Carlyle. And of course he had to put up a brave front and pretend he was totally fine. These guys could smell weakness and the smell made them bloodthirsty.

Carlyle had to shake a few hands and have quick conversations with half a dozen O'Malley associates before Erin was finally able to get his reinforced door between him and his so-called friends. When she felt the lock click shut, she breathed a sigh of relief and leaned against the door. Rolf cocked his head at her, wondering what was happening next.

"Have you considered a transfer to the Secret Service?" Carlyle asked. His face was a little pale, but he still had a twinkle in his eye.

"No, thanks," she said. "If I'm going to take a bullet for someone, I don't want it to be some jerk in a fancy suit."

"Would you prefer I dressed more blue-collar?"

She laughed. "No, I'd prefer to put you to bed."

"If you insist, darling. No one I'd rather go to bed with."

"That's not what I meant. You've been hanging around Corky again, haven't you."

"Merely trying to lighten your mood. I think I'll be having that lie-down now. Will you be going out again?"

"I have to. Work. Do you need a hand up the stairs?"

"If you wouldn't mind."

She put a hand on his arm and helped him up to the bedroom. "You sure you'll be okay here on your own?" she asked.

"I've a brigade of good lads within call if I've need of them. Take care of yourself, darling."

Erin took Rolf back downstairs and out into the main room. She intended to slip quietly out the back without making further contact with the O'Malleys.

She almost made it.

"Leaving so soon, love?"

The voice was right behind her. She hadn't even known he was there. "How do you do that, Corky?" she asked without turning.

"Years of practice tiptoeing out of lasses' bedrooms so as not to wake the parents, love."

"You keep sneaking up on cops, sooner or later someone's going to blow your head off by mistake." Then she did turn. James Corcoran was grinning at her, his bright green eyes alive with mischief and good cheer.

"Ah, Erin, I don't believe it for a moment. I'm far too quick for them."

"No one's faster than a bullet," she said. "You trying to tell me you've never been shot?"

"Just the once, and it barely nicked me. I couldn't help but notice you heading out into the cold dark night with naught but your dog for escort. Where would you be going?"

"Police business, Corky."

"And there I was, thinking you were going clubbing on a weekend without your lad."

"I'm going to a club, but it's on police business, like I said."

"Ah, grand. Which one?"

"Club Armageddon."

"What a coincidence! I was just on my way there myself!"

Erin gave him a dirty look. "No you weren't."

The look bounced right off him. "I am now. If you happen to be going to the same club, perhaps we'll run into one another."

"Don't get in my way, Corky. I have work to do."

"Don't get in mine, love. I have recreation to do." He winked. But Erin knew there was another side to his words. He was keeping an eye on her for Carlyle's sake. Maybe Carlyle had asked him to, maybe not. But there was no talking him out of it.

Erin rolled her eyes. "Do what you want, but you're not riding there in my car."

"Wouldn't dream of it. Why would I want your weary old automobile when my convertible's ready and willing? I'll race you there."

"Are you seriously challenging a cop to an illegal street race?"

"I'll give you a two-second head start," he said.

"If we're ever in a car chase, it'll be me chasing you."

"Something we can agree on."

"And if I catch you, I'll throw your ass in jail."

"Promises, love."

* * *

Despite his bravado, Corky was a skillful driver who didn't do anything Erin could bust him for. His yellow BMW was easy to keep in sight, and he clearly knew where she was going, because he never hesitated. They arrived only a few seconds apart. He jumped out of his car right over the door almost before the engine stopped, gave her a wave, and sauntered into the club.

Erin got out of her car in a more traditional style and followed. She wasn't really that annoyed. Corky was a handy guy to have around if things got rough. However, he was also the sort of guy who made things go that way in the first place, so hanging with him was a gamble. Still, she did like him, and Carlyle trusted him completely.

The bouncer gave a dubious look to Rolf. "No pets, lady," he said.

Rolf returned the look. He appeared mildly offended.

She showed her shield. "He's a working K-9. He goes where I go."

"You got a warrant?"

"If you need a warrant to let a customer in, you're not going to be doing much business."

"Fifteen buck cover charge."

"Really?"

"You say you're a customer, you pay the cover."

"Fifteen seems a little steep."

"Five 'cause you're a woman."

"And the other ten?"

The bouncer pointed to Rolf. "He's not."

Erin gave him a flat, unamused look. "You're slapping a cover charge on my *dog*?"

"Lady, I don't want him in here at all. Either he's a pet, or he's a cop. If he's comin' in without a warrant, that makes him a customer. And he's not female. Ten bucks or he stays outside."

It wasn't worth arguing. She paid and went in.

Club Armageddon was exactly as she'd imagined it. Dim lighting, flames, black-painted walls. The clientele looked to be young adults, most of them at least ten years younger than Erin, sporting party clothes that told her she'd never be that young or cool again. Corky was even older than she was, but he had a way of fitting in wherever he went. Before she'd finished sizing up the room, he was at the bar in conversation with the prettiest girl in the place.

Erin was looking at the bartender. He was a big guy whose eyes reflected the firelight with a distinctive reddish glow. She went straight for him.

"What can I get you?" he asked.

"Marv, right?" she said.

"Yeah, that's me," he said. "But I don't think I know you. I know most of the regulars. I don't think you've been in here before."

"I want to talk about a girl who was in here last night."

His face became instantly wary. "You a cop?"

"Would it bother you if I was? Have you been doing anything you wouldn't want a cop to know about?"

"Lady, I just work here," Marv said, spreading his hands to indicate the bar. "People want drinks, I serve 'em. Nothing shady 'bout that."

"Even if they're underage?"

"I card 'em."

She nodded. "I get it, the light's bad in here, it can be hard to pick out a forged ID. But that's not why I'm here. This girl got in some trouble. You're one of the people she remembers from last night. Maybe you remember her. Blonde teenager, a little shorter than I am, skinny, fishnet stockings, miniskirt, halter top?"

"We don't serve anyone under twenty-one in here. No teenagers, no way."

Erin smiled cynically. "Okay, then you won't mind if I bring in some uniforms and check everybody in the place right now. With a suspension of your liquor license if we happen to find anyone underage, of course. Not that you'd worry about that, because I've got your word everyone in here is legit."

Marv looked a little nervous now. "Okay, lady, you don't need to do that. We can talk about this."

"Then start talking. I like what you say, I'll buy a drink. Hell, I'll even tip you. This girl would've been talking to someone, an older guy, maybe."

"Yeah, yeah, I remember her. She was hot, right?"

Erin resisted the urge to give an exasperated sigh. "Yeah, she's good-looking."

"Okay, she was wearing a mini, sure, but she wasn't wearing fishnets. I know, I got a good look at those legs. Hey, don't look at me like that, she was showing 'em off to everybody. High-heel boots, too. She was with these two other chicks. One of them was seriously smashed. She took the walk of shame to the ladies' room and stayed in there for a while."

"What did the blonde do?" Erin asked.

"There was this guy. An older dude, yeah, even older than you."

Thanks, Erin thought sourly. She was every day of thirty-five, not exactly all dried up with age.

"He was chatting her up," Marv went on. "He bought her a drink."

"You think maybe he slipped her a Mickey?" she asked.

"Wouldn't surprise me. I mean, he looked like he was looking to get laid, and if he was, he'd be needing some assistance, know what I mean? Little blue pill for himself if nothing else." Marv laughed. "Dunno why the old guys look for the young ones. I mean, it's not like they can keep up with 'em."

Erin felt a sudden desire to reach across the bar, grab Marv by the collar, and bash his head into the countertop a few times. She put a forced, artificial smile on her face and reminded herself she was getting important information from this creep.

"How'd this guy pay for the drink?" she asked.

"Cash."

That meant no electronic payment trail, unfortunately. "Can you describe him?" she asked.

"Yeah, I'd say he was forty-five or fifty, kinda short. Shorter than you, but only an inch or two. Bald, but he combed it over, like that ever fools anybody. Glasses."

"Any facial hair?"

"Nah. Hard to tell colors under these lights, but I'd say he had brown hair, going gray on the edges. Kinda pudgy. Wearing a suit. He looked kinda like a high-school teacher, but better dressed. We get those guys in here sometimes, you know. Looking to score off the younger girls. I don't judge."

The urge to smash Marv's face was getting stronger, but she kept resisting. "You got security camera footage?"

"Yeah, but the owner's the only one who sees it. And you'd need a court order for that."

"What happened between this guy and the girl?" she asked.

"They talked for a bit, and then she got real tipsy. He helped her out of the place and that's the last I saw of them."

"When did this happen?"

He shrugged. "I dunno. We had lots of customers. Maybe around one?"

"And you just let a girl go out of a bar with a guy who drugged her?"

He shrugged again. "It's a free country, lady. I ain't the cops."

She leaned forward. "Yeah, but I am. I'm investigating a wrongful death, and if I come up with anything that says your club was involved, I'm coming back here. Cute place you got here, cute name, but if I come back, it really will be the end of the world. You get me?"

Marv wasn't smiling anymore. "Hey, I didn't do nothing."

"I know," she growled. "You didn't do anything. A girl got drugged and kidnapped, a guy's dead, and you didn't do a damn thing." She shoved off from the bar. Then she paused. A little thought was prying at the back of her mind.

She turned back to Marv. "You said she wasn't wearing fishnets."

"No. She was in, like, a denim miniskirt and a tight blouse. And those boots."

Erin nodded. She was remembering what Tammy had said. The girl had claimed the clothes she was wearing weren't hers. Which didn't make any sense.

"Unless someone changed her clothes," she muttered.

"What?" Marv asked.

"Forget about it," she said. "I wasn't talking to you. What's the deal with your eyes, anyway?"

"Oh, these?" He gestured toward his own face. "Colored contacts. The chicks dig 'em."

"I bet they do." She headed for the exit. Corky was still making time at the other end of the bar. He appeared to be doing well. Erin wondered momentarily whether she should step in and say something, but couldn't think of a single thing to say. It was none of her business, anyway.

It struck her, when she was back in her car, that Marv had been thinking of things the same way she had.

"I guess we're all sons of bitches sometimes," she told Rolf.

He wagged his tail. He didn't know what she was talking about. He was a good boy all the time, and he knew it.

Chapter 7

In church the next morning, Erin tried not to squirm. She'd gone along with Carlyle's suggestion that they attend Mass together at his church, but she drew the line at wearing some frilly dress. She wore what she'd be wearing to work as soon as the service ended: slacks, sensible shoes, and a dark red button-down blouse. She'd left Rolf back at the Corner, along with her Glock and shield, but her backup gun nestled unobtrusively at her ankle. She'd worn it so often, she didn't even notice its weight anymore, but she knew it was there.

She felt out of place. It was a predominantly Irish congregation, she told herself. They were Catholics; so was she. They ought to be her people. But she honestly couldn't remember the last time she'd been to Mass. She felt like a fake, a poser. And what about the man beside her, all done up in his Sunday best? He'd told her he'd attended Mass almost every week his whole life. But he was a career criminal. If he believed in God so strongly, surely he would have tried to do something else with his career. She'd have to ask him about that.

The bible verse the priest was talking about didn't make her feel better. It was from the book of James and was about patience. "Everyone should be quick to listen, slow to speak and slow to become angry." It was good advice, she supposed, but didn't really fit with her personality.

She took Communion side by side with Carlyle. He gave a slight hiss of discomfort when he went to his knees at the rail. But when the priest put the wafer in his mouth, Erin saw, out of the corner of her eye, an expression of peace on his face that she'd only seen when he was asleep. She felt no such serenity.

He shook his head when she offered a hand up, struggling to his feet under his own power. He smiled, tight-lipped, and walked stiffly back to their pew.

"That's it," she whispered. "You overdid it last night and this morning. The minute this is over, we're going back home and you're going to lie down."

It was an indication of how he was feeling that he didn't argue.

* * *

On her way to work after Mass, Erin tried to put her mind back in the game. Worrying about Carlyle wouldn't do him, or her, any good. She had a job to do. She glanced at Rolf in the rearview mirror. She should think like him. He didn't care about anything else once he had a good scent. When he was working, he was a hundred percent focused.

She found Vic up in Major Crimes. Webb's desk was empty; it was his turn for a day off. The room was quiet. The whiteboard they used for their current case was depressingly empty except for some photos of the scene and a very short initial report from Levine.

"You good with God now?" Vic asked.

"Good enough," she said. "What'd you find on the Ross kid?"

"He never got in any trouble. Perfect little angel. Went to a nice prep school, skated into Harvard through the good ol' boys network, nothing at all on his record."

She gave him a look. "You believe that?"

"Not for a second," he said. "You may be the fancy Detective Second Grade, but I do have a brain. So I started calling his old classmates. The Harvard guys were pretty closemouthed. They're not gonna talk to some dumb Russian gumshoe, not when he's asking them to spill dirt on one of their own. But his high-school buddies were a little more forthcoming. Now, Marcus Ross has been in the New York Senate for the past hundred years or so, right?"

"As long as I can remember," Erin agreed.

"What do you suppose his only child, his golden boy, got up to in school?"

Erin tapped her chin in mock thought. "I'd guess he got away with anything and everything. The school administration would've quashed any serious stuff. Even the law wouldn't have tried to touch him."

"You'd be right," Vic said. "Little Marty Ross was a serious hell-raiser back in the day. I got on the horn with a guy I know over in the One."

Erin nodded her understanding. The First Precinct had responsibility for the part of Manhattan that contained Tribeca.

"He said it was kind of an open secret there that if they ever got a noise complaint from a party, or a drunk and disorderly bust, Ross's name wasn't to go on any paperwork," he explained.

"It's like diplomatic immunity," she said. "Only not foreign."

"Domestic immunity?" Vic suggested. "That's got a nice ring to it. I hate it."

"Just a guess," she said. "Did a certain Detective Lacroix formerly work in the One?"

Vic snapped his fingers. "Right the first time. I did some digging on his background. I don't think he's dirty exactly, but he's in deep with Ross's people. Let's just say he's got a sense of where his best interests lie. He's done some moonlighting as a security consultant for Ross. He worked with the Senator's campaign last election cycle, and his name's on some stuff for the current election, too. I wasn't able to get all the paperwork from them. If the Lieutenant hadn't told us to play it quiet, I'd have logged a FOIA request, but that would've made too much noise."

She nodded again. Vic's instincts were good. A Freedom of Information Act request would have set off alarm bells at the Ross campaign and definitely would've gotten the Senator's attention.

"So how about the club?" he asked. "You get out there last night?"

"Yeah. I ought to have Brown send some undercover Vice cops in, shut the whole place down for underage violations. When I leaned on the bartender, he confirmed Tammy's story. Some older guy was chatting her up and probably spiked her drink. Then he hauled her semi-conscious ass out of there, and that's the last anyone saw of her until she ended up in the back seat with the dead guy. How old was Martin Ross, anyway?"

"Twenty-three. Just out of college."

"If he was still alive, and if she'd been assaulted, he'd be looking at statutory rape charges," she said. "Tammy's a year under the age of consent. If it wasn't rape anyway, on account of the drugs. What a jerk."

"This is what happens when you let a kid get away with shit," Vic said. "He grows up thinking he can do whatever he wants. Hell, if he wasn't dead, I'd kick his ass. He didn't even have the balls to go get the girl himself. He sent one of his guys to do it for him."

"Why?" Erin wondered. "He seemed like a good-looking kid. Why send some sketchy guy twice his age? He'd have better luck doing it himself, and it's always riskier to involve more people. We're missing something here, Vic."

"We're missing lots of things," he said gloomily. "Like the autopsy. Hell, is Ross our victim? Or this Cartwright kid? Or both? You think she had the drugs on her?"

"She might've gotten them at the concert," Erin said. "There were definitely drugs available in Central Park."

"Drugs? In Central Park?" Vic feigned astonishment.

She ignored him. "Suppose Tammy gets some good stuff there. Maybe from one of her girlfriends. Then maybe she's talking with this guy at the club, he tells her about this guy she ought to meet, she pretends to be drugged... no. That's insane."

"Ross was a wild kid," Vic said. "No doubt about it. I found some tabloid articles about him. Nothing substantiated, but he's believed to have done some tail-chasing. He definitely got smashed a couple weeks ago at a rooftop party. Made a scene that got into the supermarket rags. But nothing about hard drugs or underage girls."

"How's Senator Ross's campaign going?" Erin asked abruptly.

"How the hell would I know? Do I look like a guy who gives a shit about politics?"

"I was just wondering how this is going to play," she said. "Maybe that's why he doesn't want an investigation."

"Because he's afraid of losing reelection?" Vic smiled grimly. "Yeah, that sounds like the way these guys think. Who cares if your kid's dead, as long as you win another term?"

"Great," she said. "So we've got an anti-motive. A reason for not investigating."

"That means we've got a motive, too," Vic said. "Just flip it around."

"You're right," she said. "If someone wanted to embarrass the Senator, they might've gone after his kid. Who's he running against?"

A quick computer search answered that question.

"Who's Madeline Locke?" Erin asked.

"Either our next State Senator, or nobody worth mentioning," Vic said. "We'll find out in November."

"I think maybe someone ought to talk to her," Erin said.

"Great idea," he said promptly. "You should do that."

"Yeah," she said. "I'll just call up someone running for the Senate and start asking questions about a drug-related death."

"You're blinded by fame and power," Vic said. "Think of her as just another person of interest."

"If this comes out, it could smear her," Erin said. "Then, if she loses, she might blame us. And if she wins, it'll be even worse because she'll blame us and she'll be powerful."

"So now you're worried about consequences?" he asked.

"I'm always worried about consequences."

"Says the girl living with the mob boss."

"Give it a rest, Vic. I'm just trying to do my job here."

"Then do your job."

She glared at him, but he was right. She looked up how to contact Madeline Locke's campaign and reached for the phone.

"Locke for Senate," a chipper young voice answered. "We appreciate your support."

"Hello," Erin said. "I need to speak with Madeline Locke, please."

"The next Senator will be doing a meet-and-greet next Tuesday. If you'd like to go on the list, I can take your information. The meal is four hundred dollars a plate, but if you'd prefer to make a larger donation—"

"I'm sorry," she said. "I haven't made myself clear. I'm a detective with the New York Police Department. I need to talk to Ms. Locke about an open investigation."

There was a brief silence on the line. Apparently this situation wasn't in the call-center's playbook. But the woman rallied quickly. "I'll get my supervisor," she said.

"Good idea," Erin said. "I'll wait."

After another pause, shorter than Erin had feared, a new voice came on the line.

"Detective? This is Steve Wilburn. I understand there's some problem?"

"That's something I'd like to discuss with Ms. Locke," Erin said.

"That's entirely out of the question, ma'am. Ms. Locke is a very busy woman. She can't make time to deal with whatever triviality—"

"This isn't trivial," Erin interrupted.

"I'm sure to you it's very important," Wilburn said. "But this is a question of perspective, and from where we're standing—"

"I'm investigating a wrongful death," she interrupted again. "What's your role in the Locke campaign, Mr. Wilburn?"

"I'm the assistant campaign manager," he said huffily, annoyed at being repeatedly cut off. "What's your name and badge number, Officer? Whatever harassment you're intending, it won't work."

"Erin O'Reilly, four-six-four-oh," she said. "I understand you'd like to keep any criminal investigation of your client quiet, and I'll accommodate that insofar as you let me. But if you stonewall me, this whole thing's likely to be a lot more public."

"Are you threatening me, Miss O'Reilly?"

"It's *Detective* O'Reilly, and no, I'm not threatening you." She thought about it for a second. "Madeline Locke might consider it a threat. I don't know. But I think you'd better talk to her.

She'll probably agree it's in her best interest to talk to me. Here's my number. I'll expect a call back within the hour."

*   *   *

Erin's phone rang less than ten minutes later. "O'Reilly," she said.

"This is Steve Wilburn," the man on the line said a little sulkily. "Ms. Locke has an unexpected opening in her schedule. A lunch meeting slot just became available. Can you be at the NoMad Restaurant on Broadway in half an hour?"

"Absolutely," Erin said.

"Go to the rooftop," Wilburn said. "You're a detective, so I assume you're in plainclothes?"

"Yeah," she said. "Don't worry, I won't make a scene."

"I'd just like to make sure you're discreet," he said.

"Copy that," she said and hung up. She stood. Rolf bounced up on his paws, tail in motion.

"Where you going?" Vic asked.

"A place called the NoMad," she said.

"Ooh, fancy," he said.

"You know it?"

"Yeah. Swanky hotel in Midtown. I heard Vice busted a trafficking operation some guy was running out of the penthouse last year. Don't wear anything too sexy or you might get sold into slavery."

"Very funny. Anyone tries it, I'll have Rolf bring you his balls."

"No thanks, I've already got a good pair. I'll come along." He got to his feet.

"They told me to be discreet," she said.

"Again with the discretion? Erin, I told you before. I'm a ninja. What, don't you trust me?"

"I trust you. You just look like a thug."

"In our line of work, that's a good thing."

"Not if we're trying to quietly talk to a senatorial candidate. Look, it's a lunchtime meeting on the rooftop. Let's keep it low-key."

"Okay, I promise not to dangle her off the roof by her ankles. Unless she pisses me off."

Chapter 8

The NoMad Hotel was an upscale place in an expensive neighborhood, so Erin was expecting something outlandish. What she wasn't prepared for was an actual desert pavilion on the rooftop of a Manhattan hotel. She, Vic, and Rolf stepped out of the elevator onto Persian rugs. They saw white, gauzy curtains framing a glorious view of downtown New York. The furniture was ornate, Middle Eastern in theme. Electrically-wired chandeliers and lamps hung overhead. Most of the tables were occupied by well-dressed hotel patrons engaged in eating a late brunch.

Erin scanned the room. "That must be them," she said, cocking her head toward a corner table. The group she indicated was three men and one woman, and it was obvious from the body language of the men that the lady was in charge. A fourth man stood a short distance behind her chair, hands crossed at his belt buckle. He was clearly a bodyguard. His posture and military-style buzz cut reminded Erin of Ian Thompson.

Erin crossed the room, K-9 at her side, Vic half a step behind her. The bodyguard saw them coming and shifted his weight slightly. The woman was listening to one of the men, a balding guy with glasses. He was in the process of showing her something on a laptop screen. At the detectives' approach, the woman held up a finger. The man stopped talking.

"Ms. Locke?" Erin asked.

"Madeline Locke," the woman said. She remained seated. She looked to be about fifty years old, straight-backed and slender, her dark blonde hair perfectly curled and styled. She wore an executive-style navy-blue dress with a conservative neckline and a matching gold necklace and earrings. Her face was a little too hard and severe to be pretty, her eyes a very dark blue.

"Erin O'Reilly," Erin said. "NYPD Major Crimes." She offered her hand.

Locke looked at the hand for a second. Vic and the bodyguard exchanged glances. Vic tilted his head slightly. His neck made a faint cracking sound. The bodyguard flexed his shoulders. Erin and Locke ignored the male posturing.

The woman made a decision. She stood and shook hands briskly. "I'm pleased to meet you, Detective," she said. "Please, join us. Steve here was telling me you have something important to discuss."

"Thank you," Erin said. "This is Vic Neshenko, my colleague. Rolf, *sitz. Bleib.*"

Rolf sat next to Erin's chair. He was a big dog, so his head remained just above table level. He examined the others at the table. None of them was doing anything threatening, so he returned his attention to Erin. His nostrils twitched. He knew this was a food place, and the humans were sitting around the thing they put food on. If he'd been a Labrador, he'd have been drooling and begging. Rolf had his pride, so he stayed aloof. But he was also an optimist, so he periodically glanced at the table just in case.

"I said to be discreet," Wilburn hissed at Erin. "And you turn up with a *dog*? And with... him?" He indicated Vic.

"I don't see a problem," Erin said. "He's housebroken. So is the dog."

Vic's cheek twitched. A small but genuine smile appeared on Madeline Locke's face.

A waitress appeared, seemingly out of nowhere. "Are you ready to order?" she asked brightly.

"Yes, thank you," Locke said. "I'd like the spinach and mushroom omelet, please. With an Aperol spritz to drink."

"Eggs benedict," Wilburn said. "And coffee." The other two of Locke's guys had a cobb salad and a veggie burger.

Erin tried to quickly scan the menu, looking for something she liked, or at least recognized. The prices made her eyes water.

"Just coffee, please," Erin said.

"Now," Locke said. "What can I do for you, Detective? I've heard of you, I think. Weren't you the one who stopped that terrorist plot last year?"

"All three of us were involved," Erin said, gesturing to Vic and Rolf.

"Excellent work, all of you," Locke said.

"Thank you," Erin said. "I'm here about Martin Ross."

She was watching Locke's face. If a killer let something slip, it usually happened right at the beginning of an interview. There might be a flash of guilt, a sidelong slip of the eyes, a tightening of the features. Locke gave nothing away. The older woman only nodded once.

"Yes, a terrible tragedy," Locke said. "I've sent a message of condolence to my opponent and I've suspended all attack ads until after the funeral, out of respect."

"Classy of you," Vic observed.

Erin ignored him. "You're in a tight race against Marcus Ross," she said.

"That's correct," Locke said.

"My understanding is that it can go either way," Erin went on.

"That's a good position for a challenger to be in," Wilburn interjected. "Given the incumbent advantage."

"Marcus Ross has held his seat for sixteen consecutive terms," Locke said. "He's been in his position for the past thirty-two years. I imagine that's about as long as you've been alive."

"More or less," Erin said.

"He's become a fixture," Locke said. "He stopped serving anyone but himself a very long time ago. The voters can see this. They can see I will work for them to strengthen New York's educational system, economy, and infrastructure."

"Please, ma'am, I don't need a campaign speech," Erin said. "How much did you know about Martin Ross's personal problems?"

Locke's jaw tightened. She pressed her lips together so the blood drained from them. "Detective O'Reilly," she said. "I'm running against Marcus Ross, not against his family. In your line of work, I'm sure you're familiar with the phrase, 'go to the mattresses?'"

Startled, Erin nodded. "Yeah. It's from *The Godfather*."

"Do you recall why the Mafia go to the mattresses?"

"They do it when they go to war."

Locke nodded impatiently. "Yes, but why? Why stage your operations away from home?"

"To keep the civilians out of it," Erin said. "To keep their families out of the line of fire."

"Exactly," Locke said. "I have a husband and a daughter whom I love. I don't want them to be used to score political points. I don't want seedy private investigators trying to dig up dirt on them. If I attack Ross's family, my own family becomes fair game. I've specifically ordered my people not to look for anything that might compromise Senator Ross's ex-wife or son."

"Ex-wife?" Erin repeated.

"My concern is with Marcus Ross himself and what he has done, or not done, for the people of New York. Of course, anything he himself might do would be fair game. I wish to be judged on my own record and character. I will do the same for him."

"But you do stand to benefit," Vic said.

"How so?" Locke asked, turning her attention to him.

"This is gonna make Ross look pretty bad," he said.

Locke was shaking her head before Vic had even finished talking. "No, Detective," she said. "This is about optics and perception. Marcus Ross is a smooth old operator. He'll milk this tragedy for everything it's worth. He'll wear a somber suit and act the part of the strong man bravely facing misfortune. A little display of emotion at the memorial service, a few soundbites, and public sympathy will give him a substantial boost in the polls."

"At least three points," Wilburn said, shaking his head. "Maybe as much as five. This is a disaster for us."

"Yeah," Vic said. "I can see you're real broken up about it."

"He's that calculating?" Erin asked. "You can't think a man would use the death of his own son that way." In spite of Vic's sarcasm, she did think Wilburn was genuinely upset. He looked like he wanted to find a quiet corner to throw up in.

"Ross has been a politician long enough to be able to use everything that happens," Locke said. "Politics is a martial art, Detective, like judo. It's a matter of leverage, skill, and observation. He's already gained from this incident. I can't attack him now, or I look like a bully. As I'm sure you can understand, as a woman in a traditionally male organization, one which holds a great deal of power and authority, I can't allow myself to appear to be governed by my emotions."

Erin nodded. It wasn't fair, but Locke was right. They had to be better than the men, because they weren't judged by the same standards. Now her thoughts were racing. Was Marcus Ross the type of man who'd turn a personal tragedy to his own benefit? Maybe, but that wasn't really the question. The question was, would he *cause* a personal tragedy to promote his own aims? It was a crazy thought, but it had taken root in her brain and she didn't think it would be leaving any time soon.

The food arrived. Erin sipped her coffee. It was good enough, she supposed, but didn't taste like the coffee she knew.

"What's your view on law enforcement?" Vic asked Locke.

"The police are a reflection of the community they serve," she said. "Good community policing fosters law-abiding communities."

"Oh," Vic said. He chewed on that for a moment. Then he said, almost as an afterthought, "I grew up in Brighton Beach. Little Odessa. Good community, good people. Last year some of the local guys tried to kill me. With assault rifles. Wanna see the scars?"

"Vic," Erin said warningly. Then, to Locke, "I apologize. We didn't come here to discuss politics."

"Everything is politics," Locke said. "Whether we admit it or not. Man is a political animal, according to Aristotle."

"What about woman?" Erin replied.

Locke smiled. "Her, too."

"Can you think why anyone would want to put Martin Ross in a compromising position?" Erin asked suddenly.

"Personal animosity," Locke said. "Revenge, maybe. Or a misguided effort to damage his father's campaign."

"What are you implying?" Wilburn demanded. "You can't be trying to pin this ridiculous charade on Ms. Locke. She is a good, law-abiding citizen doing good work. She obviously had nothing to do with any of this nonsense. She may be taking the high road by refusing to call her opponent out on his son being a womanizing drug-addict loser, but that doesn't make any of it less true."

"Steve, please," Locke said. "That poor boy is dead."

"So we should pretend he was a saint?" Wilburn retorted.

"Was he Catholic?" Vic asked. "I think you gotta be Catholic if you wanna be a saint."

Everyone looked at him.

"What?" he said. "I don't know anything about being a saint."

"Clearly," Locke said dryly. That drew a laugh from everyone at the table, except Wilburn. He kept glaring at the detectives as if he personally blamed them for the situation.

"Thank you for your time, Ms. Locke," Erin said. She took one more sip of coffee and stood up. This time, Locke also rose, as did the others at the table.

"My pleasure," Locke said. She offered her hand again. "Please remember to vote this November."

Erin shook with her. "Always do."

"I don't," Vic said. "It only encourages them."

"That's a good way to make sure nothing ever changes," Locke said.

"What planet you from?" Vic shot back. "Nothing ever does change. You think otherwise, I can get you a great deal on the Brooklyn Bridge."

* * *

"So that was you being a ninja?" Erin asked on the elevator ride down.

"How much do you know about ninjas?" Vic replied.

"I know they're stealthy. Quiet. Japanese. Lots of things you're not."

"You know what ninjas did? Assassinations. I figure I did pretty good not stabbing her."

"With what? A dinner fork?"

"My knife."

Erin shook her head. "You carry a knife?"

He looked surprised. "Don't you?"

"Yeah. A Swiss Army knife. It's a tool, not a weapon. I'm a little scared to ask, but what kind do you carry?"

"An Annihilate Cross-Border Survival Knife," Vic said proudly. "I read about it in *Soldier of Fortune.*"

"I'm sure that'll be really useful in the urban jungle," she said. "You know who reads that magazine, don't you? Guys the FBI goes after who live out in the boonies, making bombs and hatching conspiracy theories."

"I'm just saying, when the shit goes down, I'm gonna be prepared."

"That's sweet, Vic."

"What is?"

"You quoting a romantic comedy."

"The hell I did."

"Yeah, you did. That was right out of *When Harry Met Sally.*"

"You're shitting me."

"Watch it sometime. You'll see."

"That won't work. You're just trying to get me to watch a chick flick."

"It might help you get in touch with your sensitive side."

He grinned. "You kidding? This *is* my sensitive side."

Chapter 9

A report from the Medical Examiner was waiting for them back at the Eightball. Erin saw it as soon as she sat down at her desk.

"Hey, Vic," she said. "Take a look at this."

"Good news?" he asked, coming to stand behind her chair.

"I don't know. Levine couldn't do a full autopsy, so she's working off what she had." Erin scanned the file. "Only one needle puncture in Ross's arm. No other track marks, none of the symptoms of habitual opioid use."

"So?" Vic had been interested at first. Now he was just bored.

"You're dating an SNEU street cop," she said, referring to Zofia Piekarski, Vic's sort-of girlfriend with the Street Narcotics Enforcement Unit.

"So?" he repeated.

"So you ought to know, this isn't how junkies operate. You think this politician's kid, a private school trust-fund brat, just all of a sudden decided to kidnap a girl and shoot up a whole lot of fentanyl together? I don't buy it. Something like this, you have to work up to."

"Not always," Vic said.

"Let me check something," Erin said. It took her a little time in the database, but she was able to pull up the EMT report on Tammy Cartwright.

"What're you thinking?" Vic asked.

"Tammy had no signs of prior drug use, either," she said. "I get the feeling that joint in Central Park was her first experience."

"Yeah, a lot of kids start with pot," he said. "It's cheap, easy to find, and you don't get in so much trouble if you get busted. We find crack or heroin on you, it goes a lot worse."

"I don't think Martin Ross did this to himself," she said. "Think about it. Would you shoot up a ton of fentanyl and park in plain view on Fifth Avenue? If it was your first time trying the stuff and you were trying to get it on with an underage girl? Whose car was it, anyway?"

"I can check the vehicle registration," he said. "Why does it matter?"

"Chappaquiddick," Erin said quietly.

"Was that supposed to be English?" Vic asked.

"You remember," she said. "The car crash with Ted Kennedy? Back in the Sixties?"

"No, I don't remember that," he said. "Neither do you. We weren't even born yet."

"But you know what happened."

"It rings a bell. Didn't Kennedy get drunk and crash his car or something?"

"Something like that. He was giving a campaign staffer a ride home after a party. He drove his car off a bridge and she drowned. He didn't tell anybody about it until the next day. He claimed he hadn't been drinking."

"I bet he said that," Vic said. "Convenient that he had the chance to sober up before talking to the cops."

"Nobody will ever know," she said. "Anyway, Kennedy was planning to run for President the next time around, but you can imagine how that worked out. The incident damaged his national image. What if that's what happened here?"

"You think Ted Kennedy killed our boy?"

"No, Vic, Ted Kennedy is dead. And there was never any evidence what happened to him and that woman in the car was anything but an accident."

"So you think this was an accident?"

"No."

"Erin, maybe there's a world where what you're saying makes obvious sense, but it's not the one I have to live in."

Erin paused and took a breath. "What if someone remembered what happened to Kennedy and decided to try to torpedo the Ross campaign with something similar? I mean, getting caught with an underage girl, both of you drugged out of your minds, that's about as bad as things can look, isn't it?"

"Well, that and he's dead," Vic said. "At least the girl lived through it. But why snatch an ordinary girl out of a club? Why not just call a hooker?"

"I have no idea. Maybe he was just looking for someone random, no trail to anybody."

"Except the girl could testify," he said.

"Maybe Tammy was supposed to die and Ross wasn't," Erin said. "Suppose they had two doses of drugs, one that would just knock you out, one that would kill, and they got the needles switched?"

"So your theory is that we've got a political assassin who killed the wrong guy?" Vic smiled. "Hey, maybe we're looking for a real ninja. An incompetent one. I'm gonna put that on the whiteboard, just to see the Lieutenant's face when he comes in and sees it there."

"That's our chief suspect?" Erin asked. "'Unnamed incompetent ninja?' We'll be lucky if we end up on traffic duty at JFK for the rest of our careers."

"So, you think Locke did it?" he asked.

"I don't know. Not her personally, of course. I guess she could've had one of her people do it. But she didn't really strike me as the type."

"Because she's a woman?"

"Because I think she's got some basic integrity and decency."

He snorted. "You haven't met very many politicians, have you?"

"I think someone was out to get either Martin Ross or his dad," she said. "We just need to figure out who."

Erin's desk phone rang, startling both of them. She picked up the receiver. "O'Reilly."

"Detective? This is Sergeant Malcolm, down at the front desk. Got a delivery for you."

"I'll be right down." She hung up. "I'll be back in a minute. Someone left me something in the lobby."

"Either a bomb or a love letter," Vic guessed. "Hell, the way your love life is, it might be both."

She resisted the childish urge to stick out her tongue and settled for giving him a dirty look as she walked briskly to the stairs. Rolf accompanied her, hoping for an outing. Maybe there would be bad guys to chase.

The K-9 was in for a disappointment. The adventure lasted just long enough to swing by the desk and collect a manila envelope. Brendan Malcolm, an old-timer who was a friend of Erin's dad, handed it over. It contained no return address. The only clue on the envelope was the word O'REILLY in block letters, drawn with a Sharpie.

Erin held the envelope up to the light. Something shifted inside, a couple of small packets. "Who delivered this?" she asked.

"Some kid," Malcolm said. "Teenager with a couple of gang tats."

"Whose colors?" she asked.

"Looked Irish to me," Malcolm replied. "And I should know." His family hailed from the Old Country the same as Erin's.

"He say anything?"

"He said it was a car drop-off. Then he left. You worried about a chemical agent? We could get a sniffer dog in here." He glanced at Rolf. "No offense. Yours only sniffs bombs, right?"

Rolf gave Malcolm an aloof look.

"Forget about it," she said. "I know who it's from. Thanks." She figured the kid had said it was from "Cars," Carlyle's nickname.

She jogged back upstairs, trailed by her puzzled but loyal K-9. Vic was at his computer, poring over vehicle registrations.

"Looks like the Mercedes belonged to the kid," he announced. "Probably a birthday present or something. Hell of a lot nicer than my first car, I can tell you that. What've you got there?"

She popped the blade on her Swiss Army knife and slit the envelope open. Three small plastic baggies spilled out onto her desk, each containing a few grams of white powder.

"Nice," Vic said. "Looks like dime bags of nose candy. You got a secret admirer in the drug world?"

Erin examined the bags. Each one was neatly labeled in marker with a cryptic three-letter designation. One said LUC, one said MED, the last one OMA.

"It's drugs, for sure," she agreed. "Samples."

"Like when you go to pick out a wedding cake?" he said. "You must be aiming to have some party."

"I asked a guy to get me samples of fentanyl," she said. "From some of the local players. I thought maybe if we could trace the sale, it might help us figure this out. If I had to guess, I'd say these are from the Lucarellis, the Medellin Cartel, and the O'Malleys."

"We can have the lab run them against the Cartwright chick's bloodwork," Vic said. "I'll talk to Zofia and see what she can tell us about the local trade."

"Narcotics and politicians," Erin sighed.

"And ninjas," Vic said. "Don't forget the ninjas."

"Vic, if we ever end up arresting an actual ninja, I will never doubt you again."

* * *

Erin went into the break room to place a phone call. She closed the door and turned on the espresso machine so the sound would help cover her conversation.

"Hello, darling," Carlyle said.

"You had that stuff delivered to me at a *police station*?" she said, trying to keep her voice down and mostly succeeding.

"Ah, you got your parcel. Grand."

"That parcel, as you call it, is a Third Degree Possession offense," she said. "That's a mandatory minimum of a year in prison. *Minimum.*"

He didn't seem particularly troubled. "It's good I was never in possession, in that case."

"You sent a kid to the station with it! What if he'd been detained?"

"A young lad is better for that sort of thing. He'd not have been facing adult penalties should anything have gone amiss. Juveniles are judged less harshly. Besides, the lad volunteered."

"You could've just waited and given it to me this evening!"

"You misunderstand the situation, darling. I never laid my hands on the stuff myself, for obvious reasons. And I thought you'd be wanting it as quickly as possible."

"What did you find out about Marcus Ross?" she asked, giving up.

"He's unaffiliated, to the best of my knowledge."

"He doesn't have connections to any organized crime?"

"If so, he's managed to keep it a better secret than most in his line."

"How many state Senators are in the pocket of criminal organizations?" she asked, not sure whether she wanted an answer.

"Offhand? I couldn't say. I can't go into details over the phone."

Carlyle was delicately reminding her that they shouldn't completely trust their telephone communications. If one of Lieutenant Keane's people was listening, it shouldn't matter much. But if Evan O'Malley got wind of a security breach, it could be deadly.

"Okay, thanks," she said. "I'll see you this evening. How are you feeling?"

"Grand."

"You never lie to me, do you?"

"Erin, I'm sitting here on my couch with a glass of good whiskey in my hand, talking to a lovely lass. Life may occasionally get better than that, but it can't be depended upon. Take care, darling."

* * *

The rest of the afternoon was boring desk work. Erin and Vic tried to track down anything that might help them find out how Martin Ross had gotten into the back seat of his car with Tammy Cartwright. Vic spent a couple of hours looking at traffic camera footage, at the end of which he angrily proclaimed the entire system a waste of taxpayer money. Erin looked up possible criminal connections to both the Ross and Locke campaigns and found nothing. She ran Martin Ross's financials, looking for discrepancies, and discovered he'd mostly been living off his dad's money. That was unsurprising but unhelpful. Rolf took a nap next to Erin's desk. She envied him.

They were waiting on lab results, a familiar detective occupation. Luckily, Levine worked faster than most, probably because she didn't have much of a life outside the lab. Erin had heard the Medical Examiner was engaged to be married. She wondered who the guy was, and how Levine had ever managed to meet him. Her current theory was that the mystery man was an undertaker, or maybe a guy who worked the night shift at the city morgue.

Whatever the state of Levine's personal life, she got results. She'd obtained the bloodwork from Tammy Cartwright and run it against the drug samples Erin had acquired. The normal turnaround for this kind of work was days, or even weeks. But that was because most samples were sent to offsite labs and had to wait in line. Levine did her own analysis whenever possible, and in this case, a simple comparison was easier than a detailed breakdown of the chemicals. She called Erin a little before five o' clock.

"O'Reilly," Erin said.

"The blood sample from the female subject contained a combination of fentanyl and heroin," Levine said, not bothering to identify herself or take part in any small talk. "By the time the blood was drawn by the medical technician, the subject had metabolized a portion of both drugs, but enough remained dissolved in the bloodstream to significantly impair body and brain functions."

"No kidding," Erin said, remembering how Tammy had stumbled into the street. "Sounds like she's lucky to be alive."

"Luck had nothing to do with it," Levine said. "Opioid impairment is primarily a function of body mass and personal tolerance levels."

"Did you run a comparison with the other samples I sent down?" Erin asked.

"Yes. Sample one, labeled MED on the bag, was cocaine cut with fentanyl. The subject's bloodstream contained no cocaine, and the fentanyl was an imperfect chemical match. Sample two, labeled OMA, did contain heroin and fentanyl, but in differing proportion. I fitted the results to a Langmuir isotherm calibration model to check for linearity of the proportions—"

"I don't need to know what you did," Erin said. "Was it a match?"

"It's a possible match," Levine said, a little irritated. "But sample three, labeled LUC, is an almost perfect match. I can explain why, if you'd like to try to understand."

"Forget about it," Erin said. "In your opinion, that third sample is the most likely?"

"Correct."

"Thanks, Doc. Send up the report when it's ready. I appreciate—"

At this point Erin heard a dial tone and realized she was talking to a dead telephone, so she hung up. "Hey, Vic?" she said.

"How much paperwork would you have to fill out if you shot me now?" Vic asked. He'd had the idea of checking subway security cameras around the site where the body had been found, on the reasoning that a killer who had deposited the car there might have needed another way to leave. It wasn't a bad idea, but the more grainy footage he examined, the more he was regretting having thought of it.

"Too much," she said. "Afraid you've got to keep living. Levine matched the drugs. It looks like the stuff may have come from the Lucarellis."

"Makes sense," he said. "They move most of the hard drugs in this part of Manhattan."

"Do you think you could call your contact in SNEU?" she asked.

"You mean Piekarski?"

"Yeah."

"And ask her what? If someone scored some drugs off one of the pushers? It's not like these guys keep a customer database."

"Give her the description we got from Club Armageddon," Erin suggested. "Maybe somebody saw something."

Vic gave her a weary look. "Erin, do you have the slightest idea how many drug dealers operate on the east side? Piekarski is one member of one SNEU street squad."

"Look, Vic, will you just ask? Please? I can't believe I need to persuade you to call your girlfriend."

"She's not my girlfriend."

"What is she, then?"

"She's a woman I hang out with sometimes. Yeah, okay, there's sex, too."

"I would love to hear your definition of a girlfriend, and why she doesn't fit it."

Vic rolled his eyes, but he got out his phone. "You know she works nights, right? She might be asleep right now."

"I used to work the dog watch all the time, Vic. I know how it works. Fine, why don't you wait till you know she's up? Then drop me a line and let me know what's going on."

"Copy that. It might be kinda late. Past your bedtime, maybe."

"I told you, I used to work those hours. If her team has anything going on, I want in."

"I'll tell her to have a cup of warm milk for you."

"Shut up, Vic."

"And a teddy bear."

"Do that and I'll have Rolf rip the stuffing right out of you."

As she took Rolf down to the parking garage, the thought came to Erin that the narcotics squad had better come up with something. Because otherwise, they were dead in the water.

"We just need a sniff," she told Rolf. "Then we can follow it."

The K-9 wagged his tail. His nostrils twitched. Give him the right scent and he'd follow it to the ends of the Earth.

Chapter 10

Erin was annoyed, but not really surprised, to find Carlyle downstairs at the bar. The Irishman was in his usual seat, elbows resting on the bar, surveying his domain. Ian Thompson stood against the wall, his position no doubt chosen to maximize his field of fire and cover all the entrances. Erin saw a lot of the other usual suspects, too. James Corcoran was playing a game of darts with some poor bastard who was about to get a lesson on just how good Corky was with any sharp object. Veronica Blackburn was in a booth with a trio of rough-looking guys. Seeing Veronica made Erin look around for Mickey Connor, but she didn't see any sign of him.

"Evening, darling," Carlyle said, getting to his feet to greet her before she could stop him.

"You're supposed to be upstairs resting," she said through a bright, artificial smile.

"I thought I'd best show the flag a bit," he said, resuming his seat. "You'll join me for a drink?"

"I could use one. Whiskey, Danny." She sat down next to him. Rolf settled on his haunches on her other side.

"Coming up, Erin," Danny said.

"Miss Blackburn would like a word with you," Carlyle said.

"Veronica? What the hell for?" Erin didn't like the former madam and didn't really care who knew it. Veronica was in charge of the O'Malleys' drug and prostitution trade.

"Business."

"Great," Erin muttered. She wondered briefly if she could make a break for it, but Veronica had already noticed her. The other woman was on her way over, hips swaying beneath the scanty cover of a very short, tight skirt.

"Be nice, darling," Carlyle said very quietly. He didn't have to say why. They both knew the danger they could be in if the O'Malleys started to get suspicious.

"I'm nice," Erin said through gritted teeth. She fortified herself with a sip of the whiskey Danny had just placed next to her. Rolf, attuned to his partner, gave Veronica a cold once-over. His hackles rose slightly.

"Evening, honey," Veronica said. "How's tricks?"

"Same shit, different day," Erin said.

Veronica laughed. "Boys chasing girls, girls chasing boys," she said. "You and me both. What're you drinking?"

"Glen D, straight up," Erin said.

"Hey, Danny," Veronica said. "Another one for my friend here, and a Devil you Know for me."

"On the way, Vicky," Danny said. "It'll just be a sec. I've got to grab the syrup from the fridge."

"That's fine, hon," Veronica purred, licking her lips. "I like a man who knows how to take his time."

"So what can I do for you?" Erin asked.

"You know," Veronica said, "some guys hire a girl, they just want to talk to her. You believe that? Couple hundred bucks an hour, you got this girl all to yourself, she'll do anything, I mean *anything*, and all they want is a conversation. Some of them are just lonely weirdos, you know, the kind that call 900 numbers at two in the morning, but some of them are married. I guess they can't get a word in with their wives, huh? But you wouldn't be up for that kind of work. No small talk, no chitchat with you. Straight to business. You want to succeed in the Life, hon, take a page from Danny there. You got to know when to take it slow. Throw in a little foreplay, keep 'em interested. Tease 'em."

"Okay," Erin said, deadpan. "Nice shoes. Nice skirt. Now what do you want?"

"This isn't for me," Veronica said. "It's for a friend. Thanks, Dan." She picked up her drink, a complicated-looking concoction, and took a sip.

"I'm listening," Erin said.

"This friend figures you ought to be earning your keep," Veronica said. "There's two kinds of girls, see. There's the kind who earn, and the kind who spend. I figure you're the first kind. A couple girls got picked up last night, slept over at your station. They were somewhere they maybe shouldn't have been, but they're good kids. I was thinking maybe you could get them off with a slap on the wrist, a warning, maybe."

"I don't work Vice," Erin said.

"Yeah, but you know the people who do," Veronica said. "Make it happen."

"And I don't take orders from you," Erin added pointedly.

Veronica smiled. Her teeth were very white and even, her eyes big, bright, and heavily made up. Her expression lacked all warmth. "I know that, hon. Like I said, this isn't for me."

"You've made your point, Veronica," Carlyle said. "Are these lasses in possession of names?"

"Bianca Fox and Patsy Minx."

Erin almost said that those were clearly not real names, but she realized that wasn't the point. "I'll see what I can do," she said.

"Thanks, honey." Veronica picked up her drink and slithered back to her booth.

"Great," Erin said again. "Now I'm getting hookers out of jail."

"I imagine you'll be needing to make a couple of calls," Carlyle said.

"Yeah. I'll be upstairs." Erin finished her whiskey. She looked at the second glass Danny had brought in answer to Veronica's order, shrugged, and drank it, too. It was a two-drink kind of night.

Her first call, once she was safely behind Carlyle's soundproofed door, was to her case agent. She used the dedicated phone he'd given her.

He picked up before the second ring. "Hello?"

"Hey, Phil. It's Erin. Everything's fine. I can talk."

"Good." Phil Stachowski was a Lieutenant with the NYPD, experienced at running undercover operations. He didn't look like much, but he'd been calm and reliable in all Erin's dealings with him so far. She hoped he'd have her back.

"I need a favor," she said. "For our mutual friends."

"What do they want you to do?"

"Nothing too bad. A couple of hookers got busted last night. The O'Malleys want me to spring them."

She could almost hear his sigh of relief. "You're right. That's not bad. Small potatoes. Have they been transferred to Riker's, or are they still being held in local lockup?"

"I think we've still got them."

"That's good. It reduces the red tape. This won't be terribly complicated. You know your Vice commander?"

"Sergeant Brown? Yeah, we've met."

"Are you on good terms with him?"

"As good as he is with anybody. He's kind of a dick."

"Why not ask him for an interview with these girls, then tell him they're working for you on a Major Crimes case?"

Erin was already nodding her understanding. "Copy that," she said. "Good idea."

"Just make sure you keep a record," he said. "Get the names to me and I'll add them to the file. It'll be extra weight when we bring the charges."

"Bianca Fox and Patsy Minx," Erin said. "You got that?"

"Copy," Phil said. "I expect this is just a test run, making sure you can get this kind of thing done for them. They'll try you on bigger fish soon."

"I can hardly wait."

"This is a good thing, Erin. The more useful you appear to them, the more damage you'll do in the end."

"I know. I just don't feel good about it."

"It's undercover work," he said. "If you're not getting ulcers and feeling paranoid, you're not in deep enough yet."

She smiled. "Thanks for the happy thought, Phil. I'll keep that in mind."

After that, she called Dispatch and asked to be patched through to Precinct 8's Vice office. Brown might have gone home, but Erin doubted it. At this time of evening, the world of Vice was just beginning to stir.

She was right. Tad Brown picked up the phone with the same world-weary, Brooklyn-accented voice she'd come to know.

"Brown," he said.

"Hey, Sergeant," she said. "Erin O'Reilly here."

"To what do I owe the pleasure, Detective?" He made it sound like pleasure was something you got when you dropped something heavy on your own foot.

"You got a couple working girls in custody?"

"Yep. Girls in cages. Just like you'd see in a bad exploitation movie. What about 'em?"

"Bianca Fox and Patsy Minx?"

"So they say," Brown said. "But their fingerprint check came back with different names."

"I need to talk to them," she said.

"What about?"

"A case I'm working. They might be able to give me something. If they do, would you be willing to turn them loose?"

"Now that's an interesting question, O'Reilly," Brown said. "On the one hand, we've got my collar, which affects my closure stats. On the other, we've got all this paperwork to get them processed, which is a pain in the ass. What's a poor Vice officer to do? I know. I'll make it somebody else's problem. Tell you what, Detective. You take responsibility for my prisoners, you can do whatever you want with them. On second thought, not quite whatever you want. Just make sure it's nothing that'll make us have to hose out the holding cells afterward."

Erin made a face. "I'll keep that in mind," she said. "You okay with sitting on them a little longer? I'm out of the office right now. I can be there in fifteen or twenty minutes."

"They're not going anywhere. That being the point of putting someone in a jail cell."

She hung up and went back to the bar. Carlyle met her with an expectantly raised eyebrow.

"Sorry," she said. "I have to go back in. Work."

"Shall I wait up for you?"

"You need your rest."

"I live by night, darling. You know that."

"Don't we all," Erin said. "Just make sure you live till dawn." And she and Rolf went back to the Eightball.

* * *

"You sure you want these two?" Sergeant Brown asked. "I moved them out of lockup into the interrogation rooms, but I don't think they're going to give you much."

"Why do you say that?" Erin asked.

"They're drug mules," Brown said. "In addition to being streetwalkers. But they're first-time drug offenders, so we can't throw enough months at them to make them crack. They're more scared of their bosses than they are of anything we can do to them. But if you want them, go for it."

"Can I ask you a favor?"

"Like what?" Brown's face became even more cynical than normal. Erin hadn't known that was possible.

"Two favors, actually. Can you make sure no one's looking over my shoulder?"

"How come? You don't want your trade secrets getting out?"

"You know what happens on the street when perps cut deals," she said. "I'm not so bored that I want more bodies in back alleys to add to my case load. If any information changes hands, it'll be between them and me, no one watching."

"You don't trust the rest of the Eightball?"

"It's just good operational security," Erin said, thinking of how Ian would have described it.

"Not even me?"

"Especially not you."

Brown cracked a slight smile. "Fair enough. And favor number two?"

"Can you keep an eye on my K-9 while I'm in there with them?"

"Won't he stay where you put him?"

It was Erin's turn to smile. "Yeah. But this way he can keep an eye on you at the same time."

She handed over Rolf's leash. "You're with this guy now, got it?" she told him.

Rolf looked skeptical.

"*Bleib*," she told him.

"What happens if I take him out of my office?" Brown asked.

"He won't move until I tell him to."

"What happens if I leave without him?"

"Do you really want to find out?"

Brown and Rolf had a brief staring contest. Rolf won.

Brown sat down behind his desk. "Fine. I've got some Fives to fill out anyway."

Erin left them there and went down to the interrogation rooms. She took a moment to check the observation gallery, making sure no other cops were present and taking the chance to give the suspects a once-over. Bianca Fox was in Room One, checking her nails. Bianca looked to be sixteen or so, until you looked in her eyes. The eyes were the sort you saw on old women or Third World refugees.

"It's about time," Bianca said when Erin walked in. "I been waiting all day, and that's after I was up all night." She was pure street bravado, brash self-confidence covering an underpinning of desperation and fear.

"You know how much trouble you're in?" Erin asked, taking a seat across from her.

"Honey, you don't know the meaning of the word," Bianca said. "This ain't the worst day of my life. Not even top ten."

"You didn't ask for a lawyer," Erin observed. This broke one of the cardinal rules of detective interrogations. If the perp didn't mention legal assistance, the detective was absolutely not going to do so.

Bianca shrugged. "And get some lousy kid right outta school, looking to put some pro bono bullshit on his resume?

He'd just tell me to plead out and go back to kissing up to the guys in the nice suits."

"You know your way around the system," Erin said. "This is your lucky day, Bianca. I can get you out of here."

"And we'll go off to Candyland together?" Bianca sneered. "I used to play that when I was a kid. You know the Gumdrop Mountains ain't real, right?"

"You're looking for the catch?"

"No shit. What you selling?"

Erin leaned forward and lowered her voice. "No catch, no problem. I tell my people you went to bat for me, you walk out of here inside the hour. Free and clear."

"Kiss my ass," Bianca said. "I ain't no snitch."

"You don't have to tell me anything," Erin said. "Think of it as an investment."

"In my future?" The street girl stared at her. "Girl, you a lot dumber than you look. That investment ain't gonna make you jack shit."

"Why don't you let me worry about that? You want to walk or not?"

There was no trust at all in Bianca's unnaturally-old eyes. "What's your game?"

"Just trying to do you a solid."

"What for? Don't give me none of that sisterhood crap. I ain't giving you shit."

Erin nodded. "Okay, thanks. That's all I needed to know." She stood up. "You're free to go."

Bianca stared at her. "I don't get you."

"You don't have to. Just try to stay out of trouble. Hang tight for a couple minutes. I'll be back."

Erin stepped out into the hallway and went two doors down to the next room. There was Patsy Minx. If she'd really been trying to get information out of these young women, Erin would have leaned harder on Patsy. This girl looked softer than Bianca, newer to the game. But Patsy still had her guard up when Erin walked in.

"No charges are going to be filed," Erin said, deciding to stop wasting time. "Get up. You're going home."

"Huh? Why?" Patsy was a little disoriented. She looked like she might be suffering some initial symptoms of opioid withdrawal. It wasn't unusual for working girls to be kept on a chemical leash by their pimps.

Erin tried not to show her disgust with the whole situation. The last thing she wanted was to let this girl go back under the so-called protection of Veronica's people. "Come on," she said. "If you want to stay here, I'll take you back to your cell. Otherwise, you're going out the door. You've got till the count of three to make up your mind. One."

Patsy got up. "I don't get it," she said.

"Get in line," Erin muttered. She walked Patsy back to the first interrogation room and left her in the hallway for a moment while she went in to fetch Bianca. Then she took the two women to the front desk.

"What've you got for me, kiddo?" Sergeant Malcolm asked.

"Two born-again good citizens," she said. "I need to sign them out."

Malcolm nodded. As far as he was concerned, he was just a gatekeeper. If the NYPD's detectives wanted to let someone go, it wasn't his problem. They had plenty of people who got arrested and released within twenty-four hours, usually for drunk and disorderly offenses. He produced the appropriate paperwork, which Erin signed.

"Now scram," Erin told the girls. "I don't want to see you back in this station."

Bianca gave her a suspicious look as she took hold of Patsy's upper arm and steered the other girl to the door. She kept glancing back, as if she was expecting Erin to shoot her in the back or slap the cuffs on her again.

"Those girls sure are jumpy," Malcolm observed once they'd gone.

"That's the Life," Erin said. "A hooker who trusts strangers ends up a statistic."

Then she blinked as one piece of her puzzle slid into place. "I have to take care of something. Catch you later, Sarge," she said and ran up the stairs.

"Nice talking to you too, Erin," Malcolm called after her.

She went to Brown's office first, to retrieve Rolf. The K-9 was right where she'd left him, his leash trailing across to Brown's desk. The Vice Sergeant had his feet up on the desk and appeared to be browsing escort services online.

"Tossed the fish back into the lake?" he said.

"Yeah."

"No skin off my nose. We'll just pick 'em up again tomorrow night, or next week. Or we'll fish 'em out of the East River. That bother you?"

"Does it bother you?" Erin retorted, picking up Rolf's leash. She was annoyed. He was just trying to get under her skin. But it bothered her because he was right, damn it. Everyone, the NYPD included, was treating these young women like disposable assets.

"My conscience used to bother me," Brown admitted. "So I beat it with a tire iron and left it in a trash dumpster a block from Times Square. Now I sleep lots better. You oughta try it sometime, O'Reilly."

"I sleep fine," Erin lied. She was seeing Doc Evans, the department psychologist, every couple of weeks, and it was helping, but she still had nightmares and the occasional flashback. Brown didn't need to know that.

"Hey, what people do in their own beds is their own business," Brown said. He paused. "Well, I guess since I work Vice, it's sometimes my business."

"You're a creep," Erin said and turned to go.

"You're welcome," Brown said to her back.

* * *

"I thought you were going home," Vic said when he saw Erin.

"I was. Then I came back."

"Forget something?"

"No, I thought of something. I know why our guy picked out an ordinary girl and dressed her as a hooker."

"Because real hookers are expensive?" Vic guessed.

"No, because they're suspicious," she said. "Any street girl who's been around knows better than to take a drink from a stranger. It's hard to kidnap a prostitute."

Vic nodded. "Yeah, you got a point. Working girls fight back. Plus, there's the pimp to consider. One of those guys sees a john carrying one of his girls out of a club, there's a good chance he pulls a knife or a gun."

"Too many variables, too much risk," Erin said.

"Okay, I believe you," Vic said. "But that couldn't have waited until tomorrow?"

"I had some other stuff to take care of. I don't live that far away."

He shrugged. "If this is how you get your kicks, I'm not gonna tell you how to spend your downtime. But you might have wanted to get some sleep."

"Vic, it's not even seven o' clock. That hasn't been my bedtime since I was three."

"You know the reason for early bedtime for toddlers is so mommy and daddy can have grown-up time, don't you?"

"Vic..." she began warningly.

"You're picturing it right now, aren't you," he said with a grin. "Your mom and dad, in their bedroom..."

"You asked me to shoot you earlier today," she reminded him. "I'm still armed. I could change my mind."

"Speaking of angry women with loaded firearms," he said, "I just talked to Zofia. She says her squad is working a case with a Lucarelli dealer and she might have something for me. She said it's kismet. I dunno what that is. Some new street drug, maybe."

"I think it's another word for fate," Erin said.

"Oh."

"Vic, is it possible for English to be your second language if you don't have a first language?"

"I do have a first language."

"What is it?"

He held up a large fist, showing the scars on the backs of his knuckles.

"So... Piekarski?" Erin prompted.

"She's on the Lower East Side, Little Italy," he said. "They're setting up in a surveillance van. I said we'd drop by in a couple hours. I was about to call you. You want to catch some Zs before then?"

"Not if it means sleeping on the break room couch."

"I've slept on that couch."

"Yeah, you and God only knows what else. Hard pass. I'll just drink lots of coffee."

"Mountain Dew for me," Vic said. "Everybody's got their chemical dependencies. See? I can speak English just fine. I got your kismet right here."

Chapter 11

"That's their car," Erin said. She started looking for a place to park her Charger.

"You sure?" Vic asked from the passenger seat.

"Yeah." She pulled around the corner and squeezed the car into a space more or less big enough for it. "Let's go."

She, Vic, and Rolf walked briskly down the sidewalk, feeling the cool evening air on their skin. Erin smelled roasted garlic and tomatoes as they passed in front of a little mom-and-pop restaurant. They were in one of the older parts of Little Italy, on their way to their rendezvous with the Street Narcotics Enforcement Unit. Her stomach growled, reminding her that she hadn't eaten yet.

Erin led the way to a dilapidated van the color of mud. Without a second glance, she rapped on the back door with her knuckles.

"Who's there?" a man said in a low voice.

"O'Reilly and Neshenko," she said.

"How do we know it's you?" a female voice chimed in.

"Because I know how this piece of shit got the holes in the bodywork," Erin said. "I was there, and so were you, Piekarski.

You want to use this on stakeouts, you ought to get the bullet holes fixed. Open up. I got a big Russian who wants to say hello."

The door swung open, revealing a musty interior crammed with surveillance equipment and plainclothes cops. The one at the back, a little olive-skinned guy with a mustache, reached out and helped her in. Rolf leaped and scrambled in beside her. Vic brought up the rear.

"Hey, Firelli," Erin said, recognizing the guy. "How's life on the street?"

"I'm buying the drinks," he said morosely.

"Wopstat," Erin said, remembering. The squad had a running game where the cop whose ethnicity matched the perps they busted had to spring for the first round. Firelli, the Italian, clearly didn't like the way things were shaping up.

"Hey, big fella," Piekarski said. The petite blonde grinned at Vic. "Glad you could join us."

The other cop in the back, Sergeant Logan, offered quick handshakes to Erin and Vic. It was his squad and his responsibility. He didn't look like much, a wiry guy in scuffed jeans and a leather jacket, his shield hung on a chain around his neck, but Erin knew he was a good cop in every way that counted.

"Where's Janovich?" she asked, missing one familiar face from the team.

"Driver's seat," Logan said, pointing over his shoulder with his thumb.

"Good to know you care," Janovich called without turning around. "I'm just up here doing my job while you guys are screwing around."

"What is the job?" Erin asked.

"Bread delivery," Logan said.

"You guys are narcs," Vic said.

"So?" Logan said.

"Is it drug money, or what?" Vic asked.

After a confused moment, Logan laughed. "No, I mean actual bread," he said. "Not money. The pizza place at the corner is a front for the Lucarellis. They get their dough, by which I mean actual dough, dropped off overnight. But Firelli got a tip that there's more than bread in the truck. We think they're replenishing their stash."

"So you're waiting for the shipment to arrive?" Erin asked. "Nail them in the street?"

"No, we're waiting till they unload," Logan said. "Otherwise we only get the couriers. If we catch them with the shit on the premises, we can shut down the whole joint. That'll give Old Man Acerbo a bloody nose."

"He's in prison, last I heard," Vic said.

"Yeah, but we'll hit him so hard he'll feel it all the way in Sing Sing," Piekarski said.

"That's nice," Erin said. "But what's this got to do with our case? I assume Vic told you what was going on?"

"Yeah," Logan said. "Piekarski filled me in. This is where the Lucarellis hold a big chunk of their fentanyl. We've got no way of knowing if they dealt to your guy, but if they did, someone here may know it. We'll give it a little time, let the street dealers drift in to get their refills. Then we bust all of them at once and lean on them. Maybe one of the little guys knows something. If he can help with a murder investigation, without giving up any dirt on the Lucarellis, he may flip. It's the best we can do for you. So, are you in?"

"Hell yes," Vic said before Erin could reply. The prospect of action was clearly making him happy.

Piekarski gave Vic a warm look. "Knew we could count on you."

"So what's the game plan?" Erin asked.

Logan spread out a diagram of the building on the floor of the van. "We got two entrances," he said. "The street door on the corner and the alley behind the building. This ain't exactly Fort Knox. Firelli, you're the local boy. Any of these mopes know you by sight?"

"Don't think so, Sarge."

"Then I want you to get a table away from the door, sit down, order a pizza. You throw down on them from behind when we come in. We'll go in fast and hard on my signal. I guarantee you, some of these guys are gonna try to squirt out the back when we go in the front, so I want two bodies on the back door. The rest are up front with me. Who wants the back?"

No one volunteered.

Logan looked around and grinned. "Bunch of action junkies. That's why I love you. Okay, Janovich, you and O'Reilly take the back."

"Why me?" Erin and Janovich said in unison.

"Janovich, it's your turn," Logan said. "You were a doorkicker in that thing at the tower last week. Everybody takes their turn."

"Then how come you're always with the breaching team?" Janovich retorted.

"RHIP," Logan said.

"Rank Hath Its Privileges," Vic translated.

"And O'Reilly, you're not even a member of my squad. You're lucky you get to play with us in the first place."

"What about Vic?" Erin inquired.

"He's former ESU," Piekarski said.

"We need your K-9 outside," Logan said to Erin. "Just in case anybody does slip through and it turns into a foot chase. They may have a rabbit hole we don't know about. I want Janovich at the back door and you near him at the alley entrance, watching the angle with the street. Neshenko, I'll take the lead. I want you and Piekarski right on my ass. Say, you guys bring your vests?"

"In my car," Erin said. "I wasn't expecting to do a takedown."

"Better go get them, then," he said. "Long guns, too, if you want 'em. Some of these guys may be packing and it might get messy."

*　　*　　*

"I knew this was gonna be fun," Vic said. He and Erin had made a quick trip back to the Charger to fetch their body armor. Now they and Rolf were kitted out for combat. Rolf, picking up on their energy, was excited. He lay silently on the floor of the van, but his tail was swishing constantly and his muscles were tense. One word from Erin and he'd be ready to rock and roll.

The rest of the team was the same way. Erin could feel the tension. Some of the squad were checking and rechecking their weapons. Firelli methodically counted seven Hail Marys on a pocket rosary. Then he kissed the beads, slipped them into the pocket of his jeans, and climbed out of the van. He had the most dangerous job. He wasn't wearing any protective gear. A guy walking into a pizzeria wearing a police vest would have raised red flags. All he had was his pistol, a standard Glock 18 just like Erin's. If things went sideways, there'd be no way for anyone else to get to him in time.

Erin reminded herself that these SNEU guys did this kind of thing all the time. Their standard operating procedure was the buy-and-bust. They posed as junkies, bought drugs from dealers, and arrested them the moment the transaction was done. It was close-quarters, dangerous work. Erin's dad had always said they were a bunch of crazy cowboys. She wondered what he'd think if he saw her now.

"Going in," Firelli said quietly. He had a mic sewn into his jacket's lapel. All the others were wearing earpieces, so they could hear him and one another, but he couldn't wear one without being conspicuous, so he couldn't hear them.

No wonder he'd been praying, Erin thought. His job took a lot of faith.

"There's the truck," Janovich announced. "It's pulling around back now."

"Give it time," Logan said. "They need to unload."

"I hate waiting," Vic growled.

"It's exciting," Piekarski said. "When you know there's action coming. Gets you all keyed up." She turned her pistol over in her hands and press-checked it, confirming for about the fifteenth time that a round was chambered.

"Truck's coming out again," Janovich said after about fifteen long minutes.

"Hope Firelli likes his meal," Piekarski said.

Erin's stomach growled again. Rolf cocked his head at her.

"Got a couple mopes going in the front," Janovich said.

"We know 'em?" Logan asked.

"Hard to tell in this light, but looks like Itchy Camporelli and Freddy the Nose."

"We ought to have nicknames like they do in the Mob," Piekarski said. "What would you be, Sarge?"

"Wolverine," Logan said.

"Huh?" Piekarski was confused. "Why?"

"Logan?" the sergeant prompted. "You know, like in the comic books? And the movies?"

"I was never a twelve-year-old boy," Piekarski said. "I don't know comic books."

"Two more going in," Janovich said. "Buggy Mileno and some skeg I don't know."

"Okay, that's plenty," Logan said. "Figure at least three already there, that's seven. Could be more. Once we take them down, I'll want O'Reilly's K-9 to do a sweep. Let's move."

Piekarski opened the back of the van and hopped down. Vic followed, hoisting the AR-15 rifle he'd borrowed from Erin's car. Erin was just carrying her sidearm, plus her backup ankle piece. She only had one long gun in her car and Vic was more experienced with a rifle than she was. Besides, she needed to handle Rolf, so a one-handed gun was preferable.

Erin and Janovich split off from the others and moved to the back alley. If there was a lookout, they'd need to take him down fast, hopefully before he could sound the alarm. But they were lucky. The alley was empty. Janovich nodded to Erin and took up a post covering the door. Erin flattened herself against the brickwork at the alley entrance.

"*Bleib*," she whispered to Rolf, who stood perfectly still.

"Janovich In position," Janovich said into his mic.

"O'Reilly in position," Erin said.

"Showtime," Logan said quietly.

There were about five seconds of silence. The time stretched out into the night, feeling much longer. Erin remembered her Patrol days, how many times she'd served warrants and taken down bad guys. Piekarski was right, the anticipation was intoxicating. Fear was part of it, but the fear only made it more intense.

"NYPD!" Logan shouted. "Hands in the air! Nobody move!"

Other voices, Vic, Firelli, and Piekarski, echoed in Erin's earpiece, all shouting the same stuff. She heard other sounds, background noise and other voices. A female voice screamed, an amazingly piercing high-pitched sound. Waitress, maybe, she thought distractedly.

"Drop it!" Vic shouted suddenly.

"Gun, gun, gun!" Piekarski's voice overlapped his, pitched almost as high as the screamer, the excitement making her shrill.

"Oh, shit," Erin mouthed but didn't quite say out loud.

The next sound she heard was a series of rapid pops, like the world's biggest champagne corks. That was immediately drowned out by the blast of what had to be Vic's AR-15. The unsuppressed rifle, fired inside a brick building, was enormously loud. Someone else screamed, and coming on the heels of that, Erin heard a soft, almost thoughtful grunt. It was an odd noise, out of place in a firefight.

While she was trying to place that sound, Erin heard flat, metallic bang behind her. The back door of the restaurant flew open. She spun and brought up her Glock. Rolf, tense and rigid, was ready to spring.

A man ran out into the alley, something in his hand that shone in the faint reflected streetlights.

"NYPD!" Janovich roared.

The man saw him and started to raise the thing in his hand.

"Drop it!" Erin shouted from the other side.

The guy froze, and for a splintered second Erin got ready to shoot. Her finger went inside the trigger guard of her Glock and started to tighten.

His fingers opened and the thing in his hand tumbled to the ground. It looked like a cheap revolver.

"Face the wall!" Janovich snapped. The man started to obey.

In front of the restaurant, glass shattered.

"One running!" Logan yelled. "Front door!"

"I got this," Janovich said to Erin. "Go!"

"Rolf, *komm!*" she barked and started running.

By the time they got to the front of the pizzeria, their target was half a block ahead and running hard. He was carrying things in both hands. As he ran, he flung one of the things away. It spun into the gutter and Erin recognized the shape of a pistol.

Behind him, shards of plate glass showed where he'd gone through the restaurant's big picture window.

"NYPD!" Erin shouted at him, sprinting after the guy. "Stop!"

It was a waste of breath. This man had no intention of stopping. He crossed the street and ran into an alley.

"Rolf!" she forced out mid-stride. "*Fass!*"

The "bite" command was one of Rolf's favorites. Erin was quick on her feet, in excellent condition, but the Shepherd left her behind like she was standing still. He was a dark, furry missile homing in on his target, seeming more to fly than to run across the pavement.

Erin got to the alley just in time to see her dog meet a ten-foot brick wall that dead-ended the alley, a dumpster sitting against it. Rolf coiled and leapt, running up the bricks. He made three strides and then was at the top, scrabbling and scrambling up and over.

She holstered her Glock and hauled herself onto the dumpster, jumped, and grabbed the edge of the wall. She did a pull-up to bring her head up over the top. When she saw what was there, her heart skipped a beat. Broken glass was embedded in the concrete, and fresh blood glistened on a jagged shard.

A man cried out in fear and pain just ahead and below. Erin gritted her teeth and swung her right foot up, catching the top of the wall. Careful to avoid the glass, she went up and over, lowering herself and dropping to the ground on the far side. She immediately drew her gun again and got ready for anything.

There was Rolf, jaws clenched on the right arm of their fugitive. His tail was lashing enthusiastically. The man was down on the ground, covering his face with his other arm and whimpering. Next to him was a plastic-wrapped bundle of something that looked like powdered sugar but almost certainly wasn't.

"Stop fighting my dog," Erin told the man. "You're under arrest." Then, for the benefit of the squad, she said, "This is O'Reilly. Got one in custody."

"10-13!" Logan snapped, ignoring her. "Get us a bus. We've got an officer down! Officer down!"

Chapter 12

"Vic," Erin whispered. The sudden jolt of fear, on top of the adrenaline, made her hands shake. But there was nothing she could do. Mechanically, forcing her limbs to obey old habits, she cuffed her suspect. Rolf stood back, panting excitedly.

"It'll be okay, man," Logan said. "Stay with us, buddy. We got you."

"Dispatch, this is Piekarski, shield eight-three-three-niner," Piekarksi said. Her voice was still pitched oddly high. "I need a bus, corner of Hester and Mulberry. Got an officer down, single GSW."

Too many things were happening at once. The SNEU squad were talking over one another. All the sirens in Manhattan suddenly seemed to be converging on the pizzeria. The man at Erin's feet was squirming and protesting, saying something about his arm being broken. And Rolf...

Rolf was still wagging his tail, apparently having the time of his life, but he was standing on three legs. A drop of blood fell from his suspended front paw and splashed on the asphalt.

"God *damn* it!" Erin swore savagely. She squeezed the cuffs tight, tighter than she should have, drawing a hiss of pain from her prisoner. "What's going on?" she demanded.

"Everybody, clear the damn net!" Logan shouted. "Unless you've got something important, shut the hell up! Hey, man, take it easy. You got this. You'll be fine. They're on their way."

Tires squealed out on the street and car doors slammed. The sirens were very loud now. Backup. The first car hadn't taken more than half a minute to arrive after the 10-13 had gone out. That was pretty good response time. They must've been just around the corner.

"I need a doctor!" the man on the ground whined. "I'm bleeding, you stupid bitch!"

"You'll get one," she said distractedly, crouching next to Rolf and gently taking hold of his left forepaw. The Shepherd tried to pull it away.

"Easy, boy," Erin murmured. "Just let me see." She hauled out her pocket flashlight and played it over the limb. The pad of the dog's left paw had been lacerated by broken glass. The K-9 was too tough to yelp, but she could tell from the way he was panting, the backward tilt of his ears, and the look in his eyes that he was hurting.

She looked around. She'd landed in an enclosed little courtyard space behind an apartment building. A couple of scraggly trees, surrounded by rings of brick, were making an effort to grow, but couldn't get much sunlight. She saw a wrought-iron gate that led to another alley and a door that provided access to the apartment.

Erin picked up the bag of powder the man had been carrying. It looked like about a kilo of what was almost certainly a controlled substance. She wouldn't know which one until she got it to a lab. It always amused her the way TV detectives tasted drugs to find out what they were. There was no way she'd ever be stupid enough to put a mystery street powder in her mouth. It could be laced with formaldehyde, rat poison, or God knows what else. Besides, eating raw heroin wasn't exactly healthy.

Logan and Piekarski were still talking. Piekarski was describing the injury to the incoming medics, presumably administering first aid. Logan was talking to the wounded man.

Erin fought her frustration. She still didn't even know who'd been hit. Not either of those two, which left Firelli, Janovich, or Vic.

"Hey, lady, you gotta get me out of here," the prisoner said.

"Happy to," she said. "You got a key for this gate?"

"Huh? Of course not! I don't live here!"

"Then shut up. You've got the right to remain silent, and I'm ordering you to exercise it." Erin didn't carry a pocket handkerchief, so she didn't have anything to wrap around Rolf's paw. The Shepherd, uncomplaining, stood and watched her. He was waiting for further instructions. The complete trust in the dog's eyes put a sudden lump in Erin's throat.

She tried the gate. It was locked. She pulled on it and it jiggled a little, but didn't budge. She tried the apartment door, which was also locked.

She pounded on the door with the butt of her pistol. "NYPD! Open up!" she shouted.

No one opened the door. They might not even be able to hear her, with all the sirens and voices out front.

Erin wished she was in TV land, where cops could shoot out locks and taste heroin and shrug off non-fatal injuries and be totally fine in the next scene. She had to settle for calling for reinforcements.

"I'm stuck behind an apartment on Mulberry," she said into her mic. "My K-9's hurt and can't climb the wall. Got one suspect in cuffs. I need a locksmith, or maybe a set of bolt cutters."

"On my way," a man said into her earpiece, and Erin felt her knees go weak with relief. It was Vic's voice and he sounded fine.

Erin shone her flashlight through the bars of the gate. After about a minute, she saw Vic's familiar bulk coming down the alley. He was still holding her AR-15 in one hand.

"How the hell did you get in there?" he asked, rattling the gate.

"Over the wall on the other side," she explained. "Rolf cut himself on broken glass some jerk cemented into the top. What happened?"

"The dipshit behind the counter pulled a sawed-off shotgun," Vic said. "Piekarski winged him and he went down, but while we were distracted, this other happy asshole nailed Firelli and went out the front window. Straight through the glass, bang."

"How bad is Firelli hit?"

"Dunno. He's conscious, but pretty out of it."

"Must be this guy who shot him," Erin said, cocking her head. "I didn't find a gun on him, though. I think I saw him toss one away while he was running across the street."

"You sure he's unarmed?" Vic asked.

"All he had was this." She hefted the brick of drugs.

"Smart," Vic said. "A Saturday night special is a couple hundred bucks. If that's uncut, it's eighty grand wholesale, easy. If you gotta throw one away, you keep the good stuff."

"That's nice. How about you get this door open so we can get my dog some medical attention? We can talk drug prices later."

"Oh, is that all that's bothering you?" Vic had been studying the gate. Now he took hold of the bars, flexed, and lifted. With a squeal of protesting metal, the whole thing lifted right off its hinges. He leaned the gate against the side wall of the alley.

"You've got to lay off those steroids," Erin said.

"Hundred percent natural muscle," he said. "So that's the guy who tried to kill one of ours?"

"Easy, Vic, he's already in cuffs."

"Relax, Erin, I'm not gonna eat him. Your K-9 looks hungry, though."

"He already got a bite. I don't think he liked the taste."

Rolf limped out of the alley beside Erin, while Vic brought up the rear with the prisoner. They emerged into a lurid light show of blue and red flashers. Eight squad cars had already arrived and Erin saw two more coming down the street. If you called in an officer down, you got *all* the cops in the area. Their captive was lucky Erin and Rolf had gotten to him first. She saw several uniformed officers fingering their sidearms and looking twitchy.

"Why'd this have to happen?" Vic muttered. "This was supposed to be an easy one."

"It can always go sideways," Erin said. "I should've been in there with you."

"Someone had to guard the back," he said. "I should've been more on the ball. I could've nailed the guy. Shit. And I was gonna get laid after this."

"What?" Erin wasn't sure she'd heard him right.

"Zofia gets off on the action," he said. "Don't think she's gonna be in the mood now."

"Thoughtless of me," Erin said. "Not considering how another cop getting shot would mess with your love life."

"Shut up, Erin. I didn't mean it that way and you know it."

The ambulance pulled up to the pizzeria as they walked across the street. They followed the paramedics inside, where they found Firelli laid out on a table. Piekarski was holding one of his hands. Janovich was moodily guarding five Italian guys in handcuffs. A sixth was lying on another table, bloody napkins draped over a pair of bullet wounds in his thigh and lower chest. Vic shoved Erin's prisoner over to join the others.

"Hey, guys," Firelli said weakly. He raised his head a few inches and smiled as well as he could.

"Hey, Firelli," Erin said. "I swear, some guys will do anything to get out of paying a bar bill."

Firelli managed a faint chuckle. "You know I'm good for it, Sarge."

"Don't worry about the drinks," Logan said.

"Where's he hit?" one of the EMTs asked.

"Left shoulder," Piekarski said. "Through and through." She'd used a couple of napkins to stanch the bleeding, aided by the Quikclot hemostat from a first-aid kit.

"Okay, we got this," the medic said. "Mild shock. Looks like it missed the bone, and it's too high for the lung. This is your lucky day, buddy."

"Lucky doesn't hurt like this," Firelli mumbled.

"Let's get him to Bellevue," the other medic said, prepping the stretcher.

"Don't worry," the first medic said. "He'll be fine. We just need to get him stitched up."

The EMTs went to work with calm efficiency, replacing the makeshift bandage and getting Firelli loaded on the stretcher. They injected a syringe into him before wheeling him out.

"What's in that?" Firelli asked.

"Morphine."

"Hear that, Sarge? And you tell us not to try the shit when we're doing a buy-and-bust." Firelli chuckled again.

The EMTs moved on to check the wounded suspect. After a quick examination, they loaded both injured men into the ambulance and peeled out for the hospital.

Piekarski watched them go. Suddenly, she turned and threw her arms around Vic, hugging him tight around the waist. Surprised, he could only return the embrace one-handed. He hadn't put down the rifle yet.

Watching them, Erin thought Vic might be wrong about his prediction for the rest of the night. Piekarski looked like she might be wanting some physical comfort.

She shook the thought away and got to treating her dog. There were plenty of police around, and every squad car was equipped with a first-aid kit, so supplies weren't a problem. She put some antiseptic on the injured paw and wrapped him up.

"I better get to the vet," she told Logan. "Just in case."

"Sure thing," he said. "We'll have these jerks at our station house. I assume you'll want to talk to them, but they're likely to lawyer up, so no rush. Take care of your K-9."

"I think my guy ditched his gun outside, in the gutter across the street."

"We'll find it."

"Sorry it went down like this," she said.

Logan shrugged and tried to pretend he was fine. "These things happen."

"You okay here, Vic?" she asked.

"I'll manage," he said, still with an arm around Piekarski. "We better keep your rifle here. Ballistics is gonna want it. I fired a couple rounds. Didn't hit anybody."

"Copy that," she said. Then she looked down at Rolf. "Come on, boy. Let's get you patched up."

Rolf cocked his head. He was fine. If more bad guys needed biting, he wasn't about to sit on the sidelines. Humans made such a big deal out of everything.

* * *

Rolf made no complaint as the vet examined his paw. He was still panting, but that was the only sign of discomfort. The K-9 was as tough as anyone in the NYPD. Erin had seen him take a full Taser jolt and come back up fighting. Pain only made him mad.

"Hmm," the vet said, a noncommittal sound that made Erin want to grab him by the collar and shake him until information came out.

"Well?" she asked.

"There seems to be a piece of foreign matter in here. I'll just give him a mild sedative and see if I can remove it."

"Isn't there a risk whenever you use anesthetic?"

"A very small one, ma'am."

"Just take the thing out. If it doesn't need surgery, he doesn't need to be put under."

The vet looked at Erin, then at Rolf. Rolf stared back.

"He's a very large dog," the vet said, his attention primarily focused on the Shepherd's jaws.

But Grandmother, what big teeth you have, Erin thought in a flash of childhood memory. "He's not going to bite you," she said.

"He's got blood on his muzzle right now," the vet said. "And I'm pretty sure it's not his."

"He's a police K-9. He bit the guy because I told him to. If I tell him to leave you alone, he will."

"You're sure about this?" The vet was speaking from the point of view of the guy who'd be facing Rolf's business end.

"I'm sure he'll bite you if I tell him to," Erin said. Her patience had worn a little thin. This had been a stressful evening. "Rolf, *platz! Ruhig!*"

Hearing his "down" and "quiet" commands, Rolf immediately flattened himself on the examining table. Even his ears went down against his skull. He laid his chin between his paws and looked mournfully at Erin.

The vet shrugged and picked up a pair of forceps. He probed the injured paw as carefully as possible.

Rolf kept watching Erin, who laid a reassuring hand on his shoulder. The dog didn't so much as twitch.

"Got it," the vet said. He extracted a shard of glass about half an inch long. A fresh splash of blood accompanied the fragment out of the paw.

"Does he need stitches?" Erin asked.

"It's deep, but not wide," the vet said. "I'll just stick it together with superglue and bandage it. You should change the bandage daily, with some antiseptic ointment. If you see any signs of inflammation or infection, bring him back in. Otherwise, he should be as good as new in twenty-one days."

"Three weeks?" Erin exclaimed in dismay.

"He needs to stay off it as much as possible in the meantime," the vet said.

Rolf looked even more mournful. Erin fully sympathized. Being benched was the worst thing that could happen to a K-9, at least from the dog's perspective.

"Okay," she sighed. "Sorry, kiddo."

The final indignity, of course, was the plastic "cone of shame." Rolf was a good boy and he let Erin put it on him, but the look he gave her was indescribable.

She drove back to the Barley Corner to drop off the K-9. They went in the back way, so Rolf wouldn't be jostled or harassed. Erin saw, to her displeasure, Carlyle still holding court at the bar up front.

"You both need to be resting," she told Rolf. "Yeah, I know. He'd give me that same look. You just need to get better, okay? Every officer gets hurt sometimes. There's no shame in it."

She almost made it upstairs without attracting notice, but Ian inevitably spotted her, as did Carlyle. His smile of welcome faded when he saw Rolf's limping gait, bandage, and plastic cone. She held up a finger, indicating he should wait a moment, and took her dog upstairs.

She did her best to get Rolf settled in with his dinner and one of his favorite toys. But the Shepherd ignored the toy and focused an accusing stare on her as she tried to sidle down the stairs.

"Sorry," she muttered. "You stay here, kiddo. I'll be back as soon as I can. *Bleib.*"

Then she fled. She could face guns, knives, explosives, and hardened criminals, but not the intensity of that brown-eyed stare.

"I'm just in and out," she said to Carlyle. "Sorry. Things are moving."

"What happened, darling? Are the two of you all right?" He got to his feet and put a hand on her arm.

"I'm fine, but one of our guys got tagged. Rolf will be okay, he just cut up his foot a little. Things got messy with the Lucarellis."

"I see. Are you needing any assistance?"

"Yeah. I need someone to keep an eye on my dog, and I need my boyfriend to take care of himself. Since he got shot not that long ago."

He smiled ruefully. "Very well, darling. I'll take myself upstairs within the next quarter of an hour, word of honor."

"You do that. And don't wait up for me. This is going to be a long night."

Chapter 13

Erin drove to Precinct 5, the station which handled Little Italy. From the moment she walked in the door, she could tell word had gotten around. The officers on duty were quiet and subdued. No cops were hanging around the break areas. She knew anyone off duty would be holding vigil at the hospital.

"Help you?" the desk sergeant asked, seeing her standing in the entrance.

"O'Reilly, Major Crimes," she said, showing her shield. "I was out with SNEU tonight, Logan's squad. Any of them around?"

"Logan and Piekarski went to Bellevue," he said. "I think Janovich is processing suspects. Through that door and down the hall. You'll see him."

"Thanks." Erin walked quickly in the indicated direction. She found Janovich and a couple of uniforms taking mug shots and fingerprints. It was a lot of guys to process as part of a single arrest, and Janovich was doing the best he could, but he was juggling a lot of balls.

"Give you a hand?" she offered.

"Appreciate it," he said. "What a damn mess. I just want to get these jackoffs into holding. Then I'm off to the hospital."

"What about them?" she asked in an undertone, nodding toward the prisoners.

"They'll keep. Screw 'em. One of those bastards almost killed Firelli."

"Mind if I take a run at them?"

"Won't do you any good. They're lawyered up. If you want to take a try anyway, you better wait for Logan to get back."

"Any idea when that'll be?"

Janovich looked very tired. "Depends. How long you think Firelli's surgery is gonna take?"

"My brother's a surgeon at Bellevue," she said. "He's the best they've got. Firelli's in good hands."

"Hey!" one of the Italians called. "I want my phone call!"

"You already had yours," Janovich said.

"I want another."

"What for?" Erin asked.

"Call my ma. Let her know where I am. She worries."

"Tell you what," Janovich growled. "Why don't I look in on your mom for you? Maybe she's lonely."

The mobster jumped to his feet. "You stay the hell away from her."

"Or you'll do what?" Janovich asked in a soft, level, dangerous tone.

The two uniformed officers got between them and hauled the suspect back into his chair. The last thing anyone wanted was for a prisoner to get assaulted while in custody, even if he had tried to kill a cop. It could get the case thrown out.

Erin helped get the guys into holding. Every single one of them had lengthy criminal records, so they were almost as experienced in the procedure as the cops were. The police moved the five mob guys into their holding cells to await formal charges, lawyers, and the usual song-and-dance routine. As predicted, all of them had requested the benefit of legal counsel, so they couldn't be questioned until their lawyers got there.

"Okay, I'm outta here," Janovich said.

"Give Firelli my best," Erin said. "Hey, where'd Vic go?"

"He hitched a ride to the hospital with Piekarski and Sarge," Janovich said. "You need him for something?"

She considered briefly. "No. I don't think anything's going to happen here for a while. But I'll hang around, just in case."

"Call Logan if anything goes down," he said.

"Hey, Janovich?"

"Yeah?"

"It's going to be okay. The medics weren't too worried. I think he's going to pull through fine."

"It's a bullet, O'Reilly. You ever been shot? It's kind of a big deal."

"Yeah, actually, I have. And I've been around plenty of other guys who've been shot."

"Okay. Sorry. I'm just a little... you know."

She nodded and offered a hand. Janovich shook it and then turned away.

* * *

Erin found a spot in the SNEU office and started reading up on the guys they'd captured, wondering what the hell she was doing. There was no reason in the world for her to stay up half the night in this unfamiliar station. These mopes had tried to kill a cop, and on top of that, SNEU had seized several kilos of uncut drugs, along with three firearms. No judge or jury in the world would let them walk. Somewhere, some ambitious District Attorney was already sharpening his legal knives and smiling at the thought of what he was going to do to them.

But she felt like she had to do something. It might be guilt that she'd been too far away to help during the shootout, or residual adrenaline from the chase, or feeling bad about what had happened to Rolf. Whatever the reason, she knew sleep was a long way off, wherever she was, so she might as well be useful.

The five men in custody were Alphonse "Itchy" Camporelli, Frederico "Freddy the Nose" Galvano, Salvatore "Buggy" Mileno, Michael "Squeaky" Santino, and Paolo "Stiletto" Stilicho. The sixth guy they'd busted, Bernardo Calabri, was in the hospital under heavy guard, having his bullet wounds tended.

All the men had thick police jackets. They'd all served sentences for a combination of violent and drug-related offenses. Itchy and Squeaky were both looking at a third strike for a major felony and could expect to do serious time. Erin started the laborious work of collating their histories, getting to know their pasts, looking for weaknesses she could exploit and ways she could play them off each other. The two-time losers were the best bet to flip. If they sensed a chance to avoid twenty-year sentences, they might be willing to talk.

"Excuse me, Detective. I think I may have the wrong office."

"I don't work here," Erin said without looking up. "The Narcs are all out. The desk sergeant can help you with whatever you need."

"Actually, since you're here, I think you may be just the person I need to talk to, Detective O'Reilly."

The use of her name, and the subtle familiarity of the voice, caught Erin's attention like a cold finger trailing down her spine. With her left hand, she closed the file she'd been looking at. Her right dropped to her hip and curled around the grip of her Glock. She raised her head and looked at the man in the doorway.

"Vinnie the Oil Man," she said in a flat, cold tone.

"It's a pleasure to meet you again, Detective." Vincenzo Moreno smiled. The acting head of the Lucarellis stepped into the SNEU office and put out a hand. He was wearing a suit that probably cost more than Erin made in a month. Real diamond cufflinks glittered at his wrists. His shoes were so shiny he'd have been able to use them for a shaving mirror and the creases in his trousers were just about sharp enough to serve as razors. He was polite, handsome, charming, ruthless, and utterly untrustworthy.

Erin had met him before, during a murder investigation that had expanded to involve the Lucarellis. She knew his reputation. He was called the Oil Man because of his tendency to slide right out of trouble as if he was covered with grease.

"What are you doing here?" she asked. She stood up but kept the desk between them. She pretended not to see his outstretched hand.

"I'm trying to help a friend in need," he said, letting his hand fall to his side. "More than one, maybe. Perhaps there's something I can do for you."

"I don't think you came here to help me."

"I find it curious," Vinnie went on. "Here you are, outside your home precinct, in an office that isn't your own, doing paperwork late in the evening. And here I am, in a place I don't usually come. It's quite a coincidence. So much so that I suspect it isn't coincidental at all. I rather expect we're on a similar errand."

"I doubt that."

"I was looking for Sergeant Logan," Vinnie said. "But I'm glad I found you instead. The Sergeant is likely to be somewhat distraught, which may cloud his mental clarity. I assume you're acquainted with the unpleasant events that transpired earlier this evening?"

"Unpleasant events? Is that what you want to call it?" She glared at him. "One of your guys tried to kill a cop, Vinnie. I was there."

"A misunderstanding, I'm sure." His face showed neither anger nor guilt.

"We identified ourselves on the way in," she said. "Your guy pulled a gun and shot one of ours. He's in the hospital right now. I'd love for you to explain how that's a misunderstanding."

Vinnie nodded and looked thoughtfully at the bulletin board on the wall. He studied its odd mix of mugshots, motivational posters, advice, and drug-abuse pamphlets.

"Last week, a young man was accosted in Little Italy by three men in plainclothes, claiming to be police officers," he said without turning toward Erin.

"And?" she prompted.

"He was robbed of his livelihood, pistol-whipped, and kicked repeatedly while he lay on the ground."

"And this livelihood," she said. "Would it consist of a stash of narcotics?"

"That's not precisely the point, Detective," Vinnie said, still not looking at her. "The point is, when something of that sort occurs, it makes people on the street a little jumpy. They may come to incorrect conclusions in situations like that which took place tonight."

"You're telling me that because some dirtbags lied about being cops, your gunman should get a pass when he takes a shot at a real cop? Yeah, I don't think so. Try again, Vinnie."

Now he did turn his full attention on her. "Very well, Detective. Why don't you tell me what you want, and I'll see if there's a way we can both get something out of this unpleasantness."

"Are you..." she began, intending to finish, *offering me a bribe?* But she stopped herself. Vinnie was way too smart to implicate himself. If she took a self-righteous line with him, he'd just clam up. Besides, she thought belatedly, he was glad to see her. Why? Word of her affiliation with the O'Malleys must have percolated through the underworld and reached him. He was glad she was here because the word on the street was that Erin O'Reilly was dirty. And a cop that could be bought was a cop who was for sale. The fact that she worked for a rival was a trivial inconvenience.

For the first time, she wished she was wearing a recording device. She'd have to talk to Phil Stachowski about getting wired up.

"I'm looking for information," she said. "I'm not a Narc. Street-level drug deals don't interest me. But I'm trying to trace a narcotics sale because it may lead to a guy who killed a man and almost killed a young girl."

"I see," Vinnie said. "And this information would be valuable?"

"If it breaks the case, it'll give us a murderer."

He nodded. "And, hypothetically speaking, might this murderer have connections to anyone with whom my people might be concerned?"

"Not that I know of. I don't think it's got anything else to do with your people."

That seemed to please him, though Erin had trouble reading Vinnie. Like Carlyle, he had the ability to put up a wall between his thoughts and the face he showed.

"Let's suppose, hypothetically, that one of the men you currently have in your power can supply the necessary information," he said. "What would that be worth to you?"

Erin knew what answer he was looking for, but it went completely against everything she stood for as a cop.

"I can't get them off clean," she said. "They shot a cop, for Christ's sake."

"What is the officer's prognosis?" Vinnie's face was a perfect mask of polite concern.

"They think he'll pull through," she said. Then she added as an afterthought, "He'd better."

"Then it's nothing that can't be amended."

"Dead bodies are the only permanent thing, huh?" The words popped out before she could stop herself.

Vinnie smiled, and though it was pleasant on the surface, she caught a hint of coldness beneath the expression and suppressed a shiver. "Death is about as permanent as things get," he said. "Let's be glad no one was killed."

"That we can agree on," she said.

"Ah, common ground. Excellent. So, assuming your wounded officer makes a full and complete recovery, which we all hope for, we can consider the other aspects of the situation. I understand the terrible precedent it can set when a police officer is wounded while carrying out his sworn duty. Suppose I were to give you my personal assurance that this incident will not be repeated?"

"You're promising no cop is going to get shot again?"

"Not by the man who allegedly did so tonight."

The shiver ran down Erin's back again. Vinnie was asking her to release the man who'd shot Firelli, along with the other guys, but not so he could go free. Vinnie was promising that guy wouldn't be a problem for anyone.

It was a strangely tempting thought. Let the bad guys do the dirty work the cops weren't allowed to do. Erin could do that. She could do a deal, release these perps into Vinnie's loving embrace, and the gunman would never be seen again, unless someone stumbled on his body in the Jersey swamps in a year or two.

If she did that, would she ever be able to look her dad in the eye again? Or her own reflection?

Erin shook her head. "Sorry, Vinnie. I can't get the shooter released. No judge is even going to set bail for him. Cop-killer's don't walk, not in New York."

"And his associates?" Vinnie asked quietly.

She took a deep breath. "If someone can get me a name, and it pans out, I'll see what I can do to get their charges knocked down to misdemeanors. They'll do some time, but it'll be months, not years."

Vinnie's smile widened. "I knew you could be reasonable, Detective. And let me say, you're doing truly excellent work for this city."

Don't push it, she thought. "Thanks," she said. "You'll want to get your lawyer to talk to the guys."

"And what information do you need, precisely?"

"A man bought heroin laced with fentanyl," she said. "It probably happened within the last week. He drugged a girl at a club and injected her and a guy with the stuff. She lived, the guy died. It was a kidnapping set up to look like an accidental overdose."

"That's a very expensive way to kill someone," Vinnie said. "And complicated, not to mention unreliable. I assume you have a description of this man?"

"Older guy, middle-aged at least, balding," she said. "I need a name."

"In the business of narcotics, my understanding is that names aren't often exchanged. The clients only want their product, no questions asked. I very much doubt a dealer would be able to provide the name of a customer, barring unusual circumstances."

"This would have been an unusual transaction. The guy was looking for a pretty precise dosage. He'd have wanted to know how much fentanyl was in the mix, and he would probably have wanted two separate concentrations."

"That is an unusual request," Vinnie agreed. "Suppose they are unable to supply a name, but can give a more detailed description? A vehicle, perhaps?"

"If it's enough for us to find him, it'll do."

"Then we have an accord, Detective." He offered his hand again.

This time, she stepped around the desk and shook hands. His grip reminded her of Carlyle's. It was firm and dry, a confident handshake. She had to remind herself that this man had killed men, and had ordered the deaths of many more. He wasn't the prosperous businessman he appeared to be. He was a well-dressed, murderous psychopath. On the other hand, he was a known quantity. She hated him, but she understood him, and this was one of those situations where the devil you knew might be preferable.

"Deal," she said. "And this makes us square, nothing owed."

"On either side," he agreed. "Though I hope it may open the door to future negotiations, to our mutual benefit."

"The suspects will be at Riker's Island until we get their information sorted out," she said, ignoring his last sentence. "They won't be released immediately."

"I understand completely. Now, I have a pair of lawyers waiting downstairs in the lobby. Unfortunately, I fear they count time in waiting rooms as billable hours, so perhaps we shouldn't spend any more of it?"

"Copy that," Erin said. As she walked downstairs side by side with one of the most dangerous men in the New York Mafia, as if they were friends, she wondered how on Earth she was going to explain this to Logan. Or to Vic.

Chapter 14

"You did *what?!*"

Vic was staring at Erin with anger and disbelief fighting for control of his face. The anger was winning.

"Jesus, Vic, keep your voice down," she hissed, gesturing around the Bellevue Hospital waiting room. "Show some respect."

The room was full of off-duty cops from the Five, waiting on news of Firelli. Logan sat by himself in a corner, one hand clutching the other, staring at the floor. Janovich and Piekarski flanked Vic. If looks could kill, Erin would have been in need of a trauma ward herself.

"The shooter's not getting away," she insisted. "I told him no."

"But these other assholes get to skate?" Vic growled.

"That jerk at the counter was pulling a sawed-off shotgun on us!" Piekarski said in a fierce whisper. "If I hadn't nailed him, we'd have more cops in the ER, or maybe on a slab!"

"And the guy with the shotgun is in this same hospital with a couple holes in him," Erin replied. "Look, this may be the only way we break our case."

"I don't give a shit about your case!" Piekarski snapped. "My friend's on the table in there right now! If that bullet had been an inch lower he'd be dead!"

"Misdemeanors," Vic muttered in disgust. "Okay, look. None of this happened in front of a lawyer. We just say Erin didn't have the authority to negotiate a deal. This was an SNEU op, we were just along for the ride. Logan was in charge—"

"Don't," Erin warned him. "You screw this up, forget about ever getting anything out of Moreno."

"Vinnie the Oil Man?" Janovich retorted. "I know all about him. That slick son of a bitch never gives anything up unless he's working an angle."

"I know that," Erin said impatiently. "He's just trying to get his people out of trouble. No kidding. And this may be all for nothing. They may not even know who we're looking for."

"They'll make something up," Janovich said.

"And we'll hold their people while we run it down," Erin argued. "Lying won't get him anything."

"I can't believe this," Janovich said.

"Hey, Sarge?" Piekarski called a little more loudly. "Can you come here for a second?"

Logan stirred, as if he was just waking up. He got to his feet and walked slowly over to join his unit.

"Yeah?" he said. His voice sounded dead.

"Major Crimes Girl here just cut a deal with Vinnie the Oil Man," Piekarski said, poking a thumb Erin's direction. "If our perps give her the guy she's looking for, we drop the felony charges."

"Except for the guy who shot Firelli," Erin interjected. "He still takes the fall."

Logan looked around at the faces of the other officers.

"Well?" Piekarski said. "What do you have to say about that?"

He shrugged. "Okay, fine."

"What?" Piekarski was outraged. She was trying to keep a lid on herself, but it was clearly a losing battle. What she lacked in volume she made up in emotional intensity. "Sarge, an hour ago I was holding a goddamn napkin over Firelli's chest, trying to keep him from bleeding out! I've still got his blood under my fingernails! And you want to cut a deal with these guys? Fuck that!"

"Why not?" Logan shot back. He got right in Piekarski's face, speaking with cold, careful enunciation, biting off terse sentences. "Firelli got shot tonight. He was doing his job. Maybe tomorrow night it's you. Or me. And we take some of these mopes off the street, and tomorrow it's new faces and the same shit as before. And we do the same dance, night after night, and it doesn't make a bit of difference. Why? Because that's the damn Job. That's what we signed up for. So now O'Reilly's saying maybe Firelli getting shot can mean something more than it did a couple hours ago? Okay, great. I'm in. You know why Firelli's wife isn't here with us right now? You know what she does for a living?"

Erin didn't, but she saw from the look on Janovich and Piekarski's faces that they did. It didn't matter, because Logan was about to remind them.

"She answers phones on a suicide hotline. And she works the night shift, which is when people call when they're really about to do it. You know why she does that? So she and her husband can work the same hours and actually see each other and have some kind of family life. She's not here, in this waiting room, because she's out there saving some poor bastard's life right now. So I want to be able to tell her when she comes in that her husband took a bullet for a reason. So sue me."

"Sarge..." Piekarski began, but she trailed off again. Clearly she hadn't expected what had just come out of Logan's mouth.

"Look," Logan said. He put a hand on her shoulder and another on Janovich. "You're my team, okay? If I could've taken that bullet for Firelli, I'd have done it. So would any of us. But it don't work that way."

"No shit, Sarge," Janovich said. "Hell, we were wearing vests and he wasn't."

There was an awkward pause. Then Logan cracked a weary smile. "Yeah," he said. "But that wasn't exactly my point."

A hush fell across the waiting room. The hairs on the back of Erin's neck tingled. She turned and saw her brother, Doctor Sean O'Reilly Junior, standing in the doorway.

"Officer Firelli's in recovery," Sean said. "The surgery went well. Completely routine, no complications. He's going to be just fine."

The room erupted in cheers. Sean staggered and almost went down under a fusillade of backslaps and handshakes from ecstatic cops. Erin felt some of the nervous tension drain out of her. She felt suddenly very, very tired.

"What time is it?" she wondered aloud.

"Not even midnight," Vic said. "Still early. You guys going back to work?" He turned to Piekarski.

"Nah, you guys go on home," Logan said. "I'll go back to the station and finish the reports. There's no way I'm putting you punks back on the street tonight. The Captain would have my shield for it."

"I got a bottle of Stoli back at my place, if anyone wants to drop in," Vic said.

"I'll take some of that," Piekarski said.

"You two have fun," Janovich said, and in that moment Erin realized he knew perfectly well what Piekarski and Vic were up to. He knew he'd just be a third wheel.

"See you tomorrow," Erin said to Vic.

He grunted a noncommittal acknowledgment. She could see he was still pissed off. But as she turned to go, his voice brought her up short.

"Erin?"

She paused. "Yeah?"

"How's the mutt?"

"The vet had to pull some glass out of his foot. He'll be fine, but he's off active duty for a couple weeks."

He nodded. "Glad he'll be okay."

"Thanks."

*   *   *

Erin unlocked the apartment door and slipped in as quietly as she could. As she turned the lock, shutting out the late-night noise of the Barley Corner behind the soundproofed steel, she became aware of someone watching her.

Rolf stood at the top of the stairs, injured paw slightly raised, accusing eyes framed by his plastic cone.

"Don't look at me like that," she whispered. "Doctor's orders."

His expression didn't change, but his tail made a slight sideways motion.

"Okay, just a quick walk," she said, retrieving his leash.

The tail moved much faster.

On her way back out with the dog, she paused long enough to order a Reuben sandwich from the bar. It felt like she hadn't eaten in days. It was ready by the time they returned. She took the food upstairs with her, not even waiting until she was at the top of the steps before taking the first bite. Rolf trotted beside her, limping a little but letting her know that a piece of corned beef would be an excellent painkiller.

Still trying to be quiet, she eased into the bedroom. Leaving the lights off, she unbuckled her guns and shield and laid them on the bedside table.

"No problems, I hope, darling?" Carlyle said.

"Oh, sorry," she said. "I didn't mean to wake you."

"Being something of a light sleeper can be an asset in my line of work. How did your business go?"

She stripped off her blouse and stepped out of her slacks. "I think I sold a piece of my soul."

The reading lamp clicked on, bathing the room in soft yellow light and revealing his concerned face. "That bad, aye?"

"I made a deal with the Oil Man."

His eyes narrowed. "What manner of deal?"

She explained. He listened carefully, relaxing slightly.

"That's not so terrible," he said when she'd finished. "For a moment you had me thinking you'd be joining the Life. Cutting deals of this sort is common enough. It's the price of policing and politics."

Erin nodded and slid under the covers. "You're right. I just don't like the guy."

"Nor should you. He's a nasty piece of work done up in a fine suit. I think it was Napoleon who once said of a lad like Vinnie, 'He's a piece of shite in a silk stocking.'"

"Harsh," she said. "But accurate."

"I suppose the same might be said of me," Carlyle said.

"Don't start," she said. "You're nothing like him."

But the thought lingered as she tried to get to sleep.

*   *   *

Erin stood in a dark hallway, gun in hand. Shots echoed off the cinderblock walls, too close for comfort. Rolf was nowhere in sight. She ran down the hall. Cops didn't run away from gunfire, they ran toward it. She passed gaping black doorways to either side. The hallway was long, endless. More shots sounded, even closer. She put on a burst of speed.

She plunged under an arch into a concrete room, lit by the flickering fire of an open furnace. There stood Vinnie the Oil Man, a smoking revolver in his hand. At his feet lay four men in the uniforms of the New York Police Department. They were face down. Blood pooled beneath them. She couldn't see their faces, but she knew they were Logan, Janovich, Firelli, and Vic.

Erin looked into Vinnie's face. He smiled like a patient shark.

"I knew you could be reasonable," he said. "Let's make a deal. Just help me get rid of these and we'll call it even."

Slowly, with hands that didn't feel like hers, she holstered her pistol, bent down, and started to lift one of the bodies.

* * *

Erin woke, tingling from adrenaline, head pounding in time with her heartbeat. She had her hand on her Glock, but wakefulness was already returning and she knew it was just another nightmare. She was used to those. She let her fingers slide off the gun's grip and looked at her alarm clock. It was a little before six.

She might as well get up. She pushed back the covers and glanced at Carlyle. He was fast asleep, his face showing only peace and contentment. She envied him.

She put on her running clothes. Rolf was at her side immediately, tail whipping eagerly.

Feeling like a traitor, Erin took Rolf out, but only for a quick turn around the block. Then she deposited him back in the apartment with his breakfast. He looked at the food, then at her. His tail wagged a little more uncertainly.

"Sorry, kiddo," she said softly. "Not today."

He cocked his head. He didn't understand. He always went running with her. Three legs or four, it didn't matter.

Erin left him there, wondering whether it might not be better for the K-9 to struggle along on his injured foot in spite of the doctor. She'd heard some police dogs just withered away after retirement, losing their will to live. At that moment, she would have given half her pension in exchange for the chance to explain to Rolf, in plain English, what was going on.

She drove to her usual running spot in the southern portion of Central Park. A lean, buzz-cut man in an olive-drab T-shirt and running shorts was doing some stretches to one side of the path.

"Morning, Ian," she said.

"Ma'am." Ian Thompson nodded politely. "Your K-9 on the mend?"

"Yeah," she said. "He thinks he did something wrong. He's going to be moping around all day."

"I was the same way after the 'Stan," he said. "Had a few weeks left on my tour, but they sent me home. Didn't know what to do with myself. You know you need the rehab, but you feel useless while you're doing it."

They often ran together. Ian was a good workout partner. He had a quiet determination that radiated off him, and if she stood close enough, she could soak up a bit of it. He didn't volunteer much in the way of small talk—that tidbit about his military service was him being unusually talkative—and he never complained.

Erin also suspected he carried a handgun in the belt pack he wore over his running gear. She could hardly let that bother her. She had a fanny pack of her own with her snub-nosed .38 in it, just in case.

"Don't you ever sleep?" she asked as they set off.

"Yes, ma'am. People only think I don't."

"I've just never seen you do it."

"Don't do it out in the open, ma'am."

"You ever going to start calling me by my name?"

"One of these days, maybe. Ma'am."

"Can I ask you a question?"

"Can always ask."

"I know you don't like politicians."

"Affirmative, ma'am. Remind me too much of the brass."

"I'm working a case that's political. You think I should be careful not to step on any toes?"

"What's the mission, ma'am?"

She had to smile. "Solve the case."

"Do your brass have your back?"

"Yeah."

"Then don't worry about toes," he said. "Just make sure you're wearing the right shoes when you step on them."

Chapter 15

By some trick of fate and timing, Erin and Vic arrived at the Eightball simultaneously. Erin ran into the big Russian in the parking garage. They climbed the stairs together, Vic holding his traditional early-morning beverage.

"How much Mountain Dew?" she asked.

"Sixty-four ounces, give or take."

"I bet it tastes like diabetes."

"Probably. Where's the mutt?"

"Home rest."

"That's rough. Tell you what. If we make an arrest, how about we bring the perp by your place so Rolf can take a chunk out of him on the way to jail?"

"That's sweet of you to offer."

"Must be the high sugar content of my drink. I'm usually dark and bitter, like black coffee."

Lieutenant Webb was waiting for them, leaning against his desk, arms crossed.

"Uh oh," Vic muttered.

"I came in this morning, bright and early," Webb said. "I was feeling pretty good after a nice, relaxing day off. Imagine my surprise when I arrived to discover my detectives had gone off freelancing with SNEU. That's no big deal, but it turns out a Narc got shot. He's lucky to be alive. And I can't help but notice your loyal K-9 isn't at your side, O'Reilly. All of which I needed to figure out on my own, because no one bothered to tell me what happened. What I'm really wondering is which one of you is going to throw yourself under the bus and try to explain what's going on?"

Vic looked at Erin. Erin looked at Vic.

"I was working a lead on the fentanyl," Erin said. "I thought busting some low-level Lucarellis might give us some leverage to ID the guy who bought it."

"I called SNEU," Vic said. "Going along on the bust was my idea. This was my party."

"You know what happens when two soldiers jump on the same grenade?" Webb asked.

"They save the rest of the squad," Vic said.

"They both blow up," Webb said. "What's the status on your K-9, O'Reilly?"

"Lacerated paw," Erin said. "He needs a few days to recover. But he got the collar on the guy who shot Officer Firelli."

"Did the lead pan out?"

"I don't know yet. Vincenzo Moreno is looking into it."

"I remember that guy," Webb said. "Slick bastard."

"That's him, sir," Erin said.

"Any idea when he'll get back to you?"

"No, sir."

Webb sighed. "Okay, then what we want to do is—"

"Excuse me."

All heads turned in the direction of the new voice. It was Captain Holliday. The Precinct 8 commander stood in his office doorway, looking over the three detectives.

"Sir," Webb said. "Didn't you were here already."

"I received a call a few minutes ago," Holliday said. "From the office of Senator Ross. He has some concerns about the investigation."

"God damn it," Vic said under his breath.

"What was that, Detective?" Holliday asked.

Vic stood to attention. "I said, 'God damn it,' sir. Respectfully."

Holliday's mustache twitched slightly, possibly hiding a faint smile. "My sentiments exactly. I don't want to interfere with your investigation, but I thought you should know the Senator will be coming in to speak with you personally."

"When, sir?" Webb asked.

"He's on his way right now. His people called me on the road from Albany. He'll be here any minute."

At that moment, Holliday's phone rang. The Captain held up a hand and went back into his office.

"What do we do about this, sir?" Erin asked Webb.

"You've been doing your job," Webb said. "Don't worry. We've got your back. Let the brass do the talking."

"Happy to, sir," Vic said.

"And no smart-ass remarks," Webb said. "Unless you've suddenly decided you can do without your pension."

"I was counting on it to support me in my old age," Vic said.

"Optimist," Erin said. "You'll never make it."

"I'll come to your funeral," Vic shot back. "I'll cry real tears, I promise."

Holliday came back out. "That was Sergeant Malcolm at the front desk," he said. "They're on their way up."

"Already?" Erin said.

"Watch, therefore, for you know neither the day nor the hour," Holliday quoted. "Let's do this in my office. It'll be a little crowded, but that may help keep the meeting short."

The elevator chimed. Its doors slid open to reveal four men in suits. Two were bulky-looking guys with short haircuts. Erin pegged them as a personal-security detail, reflecting that mobsters and politicians really were a lot alike. The other two were a middle-aged balding man she didn't know and an older, heavyset guy whose face most New Yorkers would have recognized at once.

Marcus Ross had been a fixture of state politics for decades. He'd added several inches to his waistline over the years, his steel-gray hair was almost gone on top, and his skin had grown wrinkled and baggy, but his dark eyes were as hard and keen as ever. He scanned the room and focused in on Holliday.

"Captain," he said in a rolling, magnificent baritone. "Your organization has some explaining to do." He pointed a rolled-up newspaper at Holliday as if it were the barrel of a gun.

"Why don't we step into my office?" Holliday suggested.

It was indeed a tight squeeze fitting eight people into the Captain's office. Erin and Vic ended up squashed against the windows opposite the Senator's goons, who glowered at them in classic hired-muscle style. Vic was happy to return their scowls. Erin thought the macho posturing was stupid. This wasn't the street. No one cared how tough those men were. It wasn't like a fistfight was about to break out.

Ross and the other older guy took the two chairs in front of Holliday's desk. The Captain sat in his ancient leather swivel chair. Webb occupied the corner behind and to Holliday's right.

"Thank you for joining us, Senator," Holliday said. "This is Lieutenant Webb. He's in charge of our Major Crimes squad, which at the moment consists of Detectives—"

"I don't care who they are," Ross interrupted. "I care what they've done."

"I assure you, Senator, my officers have acted entirely within the bounds—" Holliday began.

He got no further. "I specifically ordered that there be no criminal inquiry into my son's tragic death," Ross said. "Do your detectives have so much difficulty following simple instructions?"

"*My* detectives take their orders through the proper chain of command," Holliday said, placing a slight but definite emphasis on his first word. "It is my understanding of the laws of New York State, and of New York City, that its police officers are to investigate any infractions of the law." He paused. "Regardless of the identity of the victim or perpetrator."

"We are in an election season," Ross said. "In our current political climate, rumor and hearsay are weapons. Any allegations, however unfounded, are tossed about in the press like so many political footballs. The public hold their own hearing and trial, without benefit of due process or legal counsel, and the verdict too often results in the destruction of lives and careers."

"A life has already been destroyed, Senator," Holliday said quietly. "My personal sympathies for your loss."

Ross hesitated and nodded a brief acknowledgment of Holliday's words. "It was a tragic accident," he said. "Let us not compound tragedy with insult to the memory of the deceased. This is my son we are talking about, my only boy."

"Have you no conscience, sir?" the man next to Ross said to Holliday. "This family has suffered enough."

The Captain blinked. "I'm sorry, sir," he said. "I don't believe we've been introduced. What is your connection to these events?"

"I'm Harvey Bolton, Senator Ross's Chief of Staff."

"Mr. Bolton, I am a sworn officer of the New York Police Department," Holliday said, and his voice was suddenly drained of its courtesy. It became clipped, formal, and coldly polite. "I have served this city for twenty-two years, starting as a

Patrolman. I have worked dozens of cases as a Homicide detective. I have handled notifications of next of kin. I have spoken to widows and orphans, explaining to them that their loved ones will never be coming home. Like a surgeon, I sometimes have to cause more pain to the victims in order to remove an infection. Respectfully, my record speaks to my conscience."

Bolton's face flushed. "No one's saying you're not a good officer," he said. "But this harassment of the Senator is unwarranted."

"We have not contacted the Senator's office in any way, except to notify him of Martin Ross's passing," Holliday said. "I fail to see how that qualifies as harassment."

"We're not being productive here," Ross said. "What I want to know is who leaked the story?"

"You'll have to explain what you mean by that, Senator," Holliday said.

Ross tossed the newspaper he'd been carrying onto Holliday's desk. Erin craned her neck. It was the day's issue of the Times. The headline read, DRUG USE SUSPECTED IN DEATH OF SENATOR'S SON.

"My son was not a damned junkie," Ross growled. "This is character assassination of the lowest sort."

"Senator, no one in this building is responsible for what the New York Times prints," Holliday said.

"But someone in this building talked to a reporter," Ross insisted. "This article has details only the police could know."

"Excuse me, sir," Erin said.

Every head in the room swiveled toward her. Webb shook his head minutely, but it was already too late for her to do the sensible thing and keep her mouth closed.

"You have something to contribute, miss?" Ross asked with exaggerated etiquette.

"We weren't able to conduct a full postmortem examination," Erin said. "But from what we could see, our Medical Examiner didn't find any sign that Martin was a habitual user. We suspect he may have been set up in order to damage your campaign."

"Which is now occurring," Ross said. "Your point?"

"Someone other than the police knew the details of what happened in that car," she said. "The person who killed your son."

Ross stared at her. "What on Earth are you talking about?"

"Our investigation suggests Martin was set up," she said. "We believe he was abducted and drugged, along with a young woman, in an effort to create a scandal. We believe the girl was supposed to overdose and he was to be found with a dead underage girl. This was murder."

"Nothing has been proved yet," Webb interjected. "We don't have an official cause of death at the present time. The investigation is ongoing."

"My boy was murdered?" Ross asked Erin.

"That's my best guess at this point," she replied.

"I don't want guesses," Ross said. "Tell me what happened!"

Erin looked at him in disbelief. This was the same man who'd come into the office only minutes earlier, demanding they *not* investigate. She opened her mouth to tell him exactly what she thought of him.

Captain Holliday got there ahead of her. "I assume this means your office will fully cooperate with our inquiries going forward?" he asked smoothly.

"Of course," Ross retorted. "How could you think anything else?"

Erin and Vic exchanged glances. Both of them read the same thought in the other's face, but they had just enough self-preservation instinct to keep quiet.

"Thank you," Holliday said. "I'm sure my detectives have a few questions for you regarding your son's movements prior to the incident. They'll be happy to talk to you in Major Crimes. I'll be in my office if I can be of any further assistance."

With that, he stood up and offered his hand to Ross, who glowered at him but took it in the shortest handshake Erin had ever seen. Then the entourage filed out of Holliday's office, spilling into the open space of Major Crimes.

"It must be Madeline Locke," Ross said. "That woman has been trying to destroy me for years."

"I understand she has motive," Webb said. "Do you have any evidence that she might be behind this?"

Ross glared at the detectives. "That's your job. That's what your department's budget pays for."

"When's the last time you saw Martin?" Erin asked.

Ross took a moment to think. "Four days... maybe five. What was my schedule last week, Harv?"

Bolton pulled out his Smartphone to look up the Senator's itinerary. "Starting from what day, sir?" he asked.

"Did anyone see him the day before he was found?" Erin asked.

Ross and his Chief of Staff looked at each other. Both of them shrugged. Erin sighed inwardly.

"He was a grown man, Miss... whoever you are," Ross said. "I haven't been in the habit of hovering over my boy. He's quite capable of making his own decisions."

"Where was he living?" she asked.

"At my New York apartment."

"He was found in the back of his Mercedes. Where is that car usually kept?"

"At the underground garage at the apartment."

"How did he get the car?"

"It was a college graduation present. How is this relevant?"

"Anything you can tell us may help," she said. "Does this apartment have any live-in staff?"

"No." Ross shook his head. "I don't spend much time in the city. I have a cleaning woman who comes weekly."

"Did Martin have a girlfriend? Someone special in his life?"

"I don't know. He hadn't told me about anyone."

"Did he like to go out in the evenings? To clubs, that sort of thing?"

Ross frowned at her. "Miss, I'm sure you read the supermarket tabloids. They are all too eager to report that sort of thing."

"I actually don't," Erin said, a little needled by the assumption. "Do you think Martin was likely to have been at a club that night?"

He sighed. "Yes, it's likely."

"Were his movements known?" Webb asked.

"I told you, I don't... didn't hover."

"He's not talking about whether you knew," Erin explained. "We need to know if his schedule was publicized. Did he have set patterns?"

"I suppose he had regular haunts. Everyone has patterns."

"Did he have a security detail?" Vic asked, cocking his head at Ross's own goons.

"Of course not," Ross said. "Martin was not a public figure. I am a Senator, young man. I am not the President of the United States. To use state funds for lap-dogs who nip at the heels of my family would be a waste." He paused. "Under normal circumstances, that is. I can, of course, see the value in a retroactive sense."

"Senator," Bolton said. "We have that morning meeting with the Teamsters representative in less than an hour. We really do need to be going."

"Oh yes, the Teamsters," Ross said. "Valuable voting bloc. Great people, they do really excellent work for this city. They've been leaning toward Locke, but there's a chance to win them over. What's the name of the fellow we're meeting with again?"

Bolton was already looking at his phone. "Ah... Corcoran, sir. James Corcoran."

A sound escaped Erin. It wasn't exactly a laugh, or a cry of surprise, but something in between. She tried to cover it up by feigning a coughing fit.

"Well, Detectives," Ross said, sparing Erin a brief, curious glance. "I do need to be going. I look forward to seeing your prompt resolution of this matter."

"Thank you for coming in, Senator," Webb said. He shook hands with Ross, who ignored Erin and Vic as he walked to the elevator.

"You all right there, Erin?" Vic asked. "You need a glass of water or something?"

"I'm fine," she said. "Just had something go down the wrong pipe."

"I'll bet," Vic said. He grinned, and Erin knew he'd recognized the name, too. "So Ross is trying to get in bed with the O'Malleys, huh?"

"With the Teamsters," Webb corrected. "And I wish him luck. They've been voting against Ross every election. They're blue-collar and he's Management, through and through. I doubt his pockets are deep enough to bribe them over to his side."

"Ross was lying to us," Erin said.

"Huh? About what?" Webb's eyebrows went up.

"About Martin not being a drug user."

"But Martin wasn't a drug user," he reminded her.

"But Ross didn't know that," she said. "He wanted to stop our investigation right up until I said we thought it was a homicide. Then he wanted instant results. He was more worried about how it would look in the press than about knowing what really happened."

"Politicians," Vic said. He used the word like an obscenity.

"Be thankful for them," Webb said. "Without them and lawyers, who would cops have to hate?"

"Criminals?" Vic suggested. "Civilians?"

"We protect the civilians," Erin said.

"Does that mean I've gotta love 'em now? I'm pretty sure that's not in the Patrol Guide."

"Like you've ever read the Patrol Guide," she said.

"It's in the Bible," Webb said. "Jesus told us to love our neighbors."

"I'm more of an Old Testament guy," Vic said. "I'd rather find someone to smite."

Chapter 16

Erin's phone rang half an hour after Senator Ross had left the building. Her screen showed an unknown number.

"O'Reilly," she said, ready for anything from a telemarketing scam to a death threat.

"Got a message for you," said a male voice she didn't recognize. The guy was a New Yorker, young, probably from the street.

"Who is this?" she asked.

"Friend of a friend. The guy you're lookin' for drives a silver Escalade. He's a white dude, maybe fifty, losin' his hair. Brown hair, what's left of it. He's fat, was wearin' a dark suit with a blue tie. Black coat, or maybe dark blue."

Erin was frantically scribbling down the description. "Did your guy get the plates on the car?"

"What you think this is, lady, America's Most Wanted? Your boy was real specific 'bout what he wanted. Said he needed two bags, one with enough to knock a guy out overnight, the other with about four hits that'd make a girl real happy. That's how come this friend remembers it. Nobody orders shit that way. They just want their dime bag and no small talk."

"Could this friend pick the buyer out of a lineup?"

"He would if he came into a police station, which he ain't gonna do."

"I don't suppose he got a name on this guy?"

"Nah, but he did say there was a sticker on the back of the dude's car. Saw it while he was drivin' away."

"What'd the sticker say?"

"Hell if I know. One of them political stickers. Red white and blue bullshit."

"And you think that's enough to get your buddies out of trouble?"

"I don't think nothin', lady. Just doin' what I'm told." The words were immediately followed by a dial tone.

"What was that all about?" Vic asked as Erin put her phone down.

She was already standing up. "Tip from our Italian buddies."

"We have our guy?" he asked hopefully.

"No, just a car make and model."

Vic deflated again. "No plates?"

"Nope."

"What the hell good is that?"

"I'll know once I check the traffic cams around Fifth Avenue," she said.

"Bit of a long shot," Webb observed.

"When you're down on points and the clock's running out, you take the long shot," Vic said.

Traffic cameras were popular targets for conspiracy theorists and viewers of prime-time cop shows. Like sketch artists, cameras' usefulness was highly overrated in Erin's experience. But she got in touch with New York's Transit Authority anyway and asked them to send the footage from the night of Martin Ross's death.

Getting the video was the quick and easy part. Then came the tedium.

"Who wants to help with this?" she asked.

"Wrong question," Webb said. "A detective should know better."

"Okay, who's willing to help?" she corrected herself.

"Let me get another Mountain Dew from downstairs," Vic said. "And maybe some Twinkies."

"Don't those things have a shelf life of a couple of years?" she asked. "You sure you want those in your body?"

"That's a myth," he said. "After about four weeks, the sponge cake turns hard as a rock."

"And that tells me more than I needed to know about your grocery habits," she said to his retreating back. He raised one hand and flipped her off without even turning around.

Looking for a silver SUV on a fast-forwarded black-and-white nighttime video feed put a strain on Erin's patience and eyeballs. Vic, armed with the description she'd given him, was watching the video from the other side of the murder site. Erin hoped and assumed the killer would have parked within a block of where he'd dumped the Mercedes.

She took down the plates of every car matching the approximate description of the target vehicle that drove away after Martin's estimated time of death. The numbers rapidly filled two pages of her notebook. Muttered profanity from the direction of Vic's desk told her he was doing pretty much the same thing.

"How big a window do you want?" he asked.

"Our guy wouldn't have wanted to hang around long," she said. "The safest thing for him to do was get out ASAP. Let's give it three hours."

"Three hours is ASAP for you?"

"I'm casting a wide net."

When they were finally done watching, then it was time to run the plates. Unfortunately, Erin's camera caught the front of the cars, so the tip about the political sticker didn't help her narrow it down. As she started feeding letters and numbers into her computer, she was uncomfortably aware that their guy might have used a different vehicle, or taken public transportation, in which case this was all just wasted effort.

Her dad had once said, *"Ninety percent of police work is wasting your time. The other ten percent is important. The problem is, you don't know which is which until you get to the end. So you always gotta put in the work, kiddo. No shortcuts on the Job. Sometimes you just need to get off your ass and knock on all the doors."*

Each license plate was registered to a car owner. Those names had to be cross-checked for criminal records, which was fairly easy in the police database, and political affiliation, which wasn't.

"How come we don't have party membership listed in our system?" she asked no one in particular.

"Because then we'd be the Gestapo," Webb said wearily. "And it'd be a short step to rounding up political opponents every election cycle."

"Hell with the voters," Vic said. "Why don't we go straight to the source and arrest the candidates?"

"Or their staff," Erin said quietly. She was staring at the name she'd just brought up on her screen. She called up his driver's license photo to be sure.

The face of Steve Wilburn, Madeline Locke's campaign manager, stared back at her.

"Got you, you son of a bitch," she said quietly.

*   *   *

Madeline Locke's campaign headquarters was in a downtown office building on Fifth Avenue near Rockefeller Center. Vic drove Webb in his Taurus, while Erin drove solo in her Charger. She felt the emptiness of the dog compartment in the back, like the gap in her mouth when she'd lost one of her teeth as a kid. She'd ridden with Rolf every day for years. It wasn't supposed to be like this. He should be in on the chase.

They parked in police spaces and met up in the lobby. Vic looked pleased. Webb had a strained, tense look on his face.

"You know this isn't anywhere near enough evidence to indict," the Lieutenant said while they waited for the elevator.

"I know," Erin said.

"I could hang him out an upstairs window by the ankles," Vic suggested.

"That sort of confession would be inadmissible," Webb said.

"And illegal," Erin added.

"Aw, c'mon," Vic said. "I wouldn't drop him."

"He's kind of pudgy," she said.

"I can bench press three hundred pounds," he said.

"I can't believe I have to say this," Webb said. "But as ranking officer, I am ordering you not to dangle anyone out of windows. No matter how much they deserve it."

"You gotta suck the fun out of everything, sir," Vic said.

"That's the rules," Webb said. "Once you make Sergeant, you're not allowed to have fun. By the time you hit Lieutenant, that's not enough and you have to take away everyone else's, too."

"What about when you're promoted to Captain?" Erin asked.

"By then you hate the whole world and everyone in it."

"I guess I'd make a good Captain," Vic said as the elevator doors slid open. "I got a head start on the hatred thing."

"Why don't you take it up with Holliday when we get back to the Eightball?" Erin suggested.

"Nah, I like my job. I'd never want to be Captain. When's the last time you think Holliday got to punch anybody?"

"He wanted to punch Senator Ross," Erin said.

Webb pushed the button for the tenth floor. "If I punched someone every time I wanted to, Neshenko would have perpetual black eyes and no front teeth. It pains me to say it, but Neshenko's right. Authority figures have power, but we have to give up fun if we want to keep it."

They got off the elevator into an open office space. Desks and folding tables were everywhere, covered with papers, pamphlets, and campaign information. Smiling pictures of Madeline Locke looked down on a small army of staffers, volunteers, and political operatives. On one side of the room, next to a table covered with plates of fruit and cookies, Locke herself was talking to Steve Wilburn.

A perky college-age girl appeared, seemingly out of nowhere, in front of them. She gave them a bright, enthusiastic smile.

"Hi! Welcome! Glad you could join us! Here's your buttons. Refreshments on that table over there by the wall. We've got envelope-stuffing for the mailing there, phone bank in the back corner. It's so great to have so many good people coming out!"

Before they could get a word in, Erin, Vic, and Webb were holding red, white, and blue LOCKE FOR NEW YORK campaign buttons.

"I'm sorry, young lady," Webb began.

"Oh, it's Jenny," she said, extending a hand. "And you are?"

"Lieutenant Webb, NYPD. We need to talk to Mr. Wilburn."

Jenny laughed. Webb didn't even crack a smile. He flipped open his wallet to show his gold shield.

"Um... really?" Jenny said. Her smile faltered. "What's going on?"

"That's something we need to discuss with Mr. Wilburn," Erin said. "Now, if you'll excuse us."

Jenny trailed after them as they crossed the room, threading their way through the campaign workers. As they went, activity ceased and murmurs began to ripple among the staffers.

Locke saw them approaching. Wilburn didn't notice right away. His head was buried behind a color printout of some chart or other. The candidate raised an eyebrow.

"Detective O'Reilly, isn't it?" Locke said.

"That's right, ma'am," Erin said. "This is Lieutenant Webb. You'll remember Detective Neshenko."

"He has a distinctive face," Locke agreed, giving Vic a quick once-over. She offered her hand to Webb. "Lieutenant. What can I do for you? I assume this has something to do with Martin Ross?"

"We're actually not here to talk to you, ma'am," Webb said.

"Then I'm going to ask you to please take your business elsewhere," Wilburn said. "The next State Senator is very busy today, and you don't have an appointment."

"We don't need an appointment to interrogate a murderer," Erin said.

Dead silence fell. In the sudden stillness, Erin could feel every eye in the room on her.

"You're accusing Ms. Locke of *murder*?" Wilburn exclaimed. "You're out of your mind!"

"No one's accusing her of anything," Webb said.

"We're accusing you," Erin said to Wilburn.

"I don't understand," Locke said. "Steve, what are they talking about?"

"I have no idea," Wilburn said. "Clearly they've got some sort of half-baked idea about the Ross kid's death. I've already explained, his death hurts our campaign. Why would I want to kill him?"

"You didn't want to," Erin said. "You meant to kill Tammy Cartwright."

"I don't even know anyone with that name!" he snapped. "This is crazy!"

"I know you don't know her," she said. "That was the point. You were looking for a complete stranger, someone who couldn't be connected with you. You found her at Club Armageddon. A teenager, drinking under a fake ID. You didn't want a street hustler. Girls who make their living on the street know how to spot a predator. They're survivors. They know better than to take a drink from a guy they just met. Plus, they've got protection. You wanted a wide-eyed innocent, someone who didn't know any better."

Wilburn was staring at her. "You're nuts," he said. "Delusional. Are the rest of you listening to this?"

"Yeah," Vic said. "We are."

"You knew Martin Ross had a reputation as a party animal," Erin went on. "So if he was found, drugged out of his mind, in the backseat of a car on Fifth Avenue, with an underage hooker, the scandal would be enormous. It might even drive Marcus Ross out of the race. Of course, the girl would testify she didn't know Ross, that the whole thing was a setup. But what if the girl didn't survive? Then it would just be Martin's word, and who'd listen to a kid who'd just been found with a dead girl in his lap?"

"Steve," Locke said. "Tell me you had nothing to do with this."

"Of course I didn't!" Wilburn snapped. "This is defamation! Harassment!"

"You bought the fentanyl from a dealer in Little Italy," Erin said, talking right over him. "He didn't know you, but he ID'd your car. The same car we have on film driving away from the place you dumped Martin and Tammy. You asked him for two separate doses, one light, one heavy. That shows you intended to overdose one of your victims."

"So now I'm a drug dealer, too?" Wilburn retorted.

"Of course you aren't," she said. "You don't know the first thing about heroin and fentanyl. That's why you got the dosages switched. It's an easy mistake for a beginner to make. You can't always tell how much a street drug has been cut, and what else is in the mix."

Wilburn didn't say anything.

"Martin went out clubbing," she continued. "You spiked his drink, just like you did Tammy's. We wouldn't have been able to prove that until today, because we didn't have access to his bloodwork. But Senator Ross is now cooperating with the investigation and he's agreed to allow us to perform an autopsy. I bet we'll find other drugs in Martin's system, just like in Tammy's. You got Martin's car keys. You drugged them both and put them in the back seat, staged in a sexually suggestive position. Then you drove his car to a nice, conspicuous spot on Fifth Avenue and dumped it. You'd stashed your own car there for an easy getaway, so you left them there."

"This is ludicrous," Wilburn said, finding his voice. "You can't believe that! This is just a string of conjectures, a crazy conspiracy theory! It's what you find on opposition websites! I suppose next you'll tell me I'm a pedophile, or I'm talking to aliens, or I've got Elvis locked in my basement!"

"Do you?" Vic asked. No one paid any attention to him.

"You've got no evidence for any of this!" Wilburn went on. "No proof. Nothing!"

"We've got your car on video leaving the crime scene," Erin said quietly. "And we've got Tammy Cartwright, alive, who remembers the man who talked to her in the club. Not to mention the guy who sold you the drugs." This was ninety percent bluff. Tammy's memory of the evening was pretty scrambled and the bartender wouldn't likely be testifying, but she saw no need to mention that to Wilburn.

"Seems like kind of a lot of evidence to me," Vic added.

"It's plenty to get us a warrant for your car," Webb said. "And to fingerprint you. I'm sure you thought you were being careful, but how sure are you that you didn't leave a print in Ross's Mercedes? And then there's the matter of DNA, and fibers. But maybe you're not familiar with that branch of forensics. O'Reilly, please explain the principle of transference to Mr. Wilburn."

"When you touch something, you get it on you and you get you on it," Erin explained. "Fibers, skin cells, everything. If you were in that car, we'll know it."

Wilburn looked from Erin to Webb to Vic. Then he looked at his employer. He licked his lips. "Ma'am," he said, but his throat was dry and his voice cracked as he said it.

Locke was staring at him. "Steve," she whispered. "How could you do this? Why?"

"Don't you understand?" he pleaded, and Erin knew they had him. "Ross was going to win. *Again.* He just stays in his office, year after year, and nothing changes. You can make a difference, a real difference. You can make everyone's life better. Your education initiatives, your tax credits, all of it!"

"By killing an innocent teenage girl?" Locke shot back. "What kind of monster do you think I am?"

"She wasn't supposed to die!" Wilburn said. "The needles got mixed up! I was nervous, I was scared! I got confused!"

"So you only intended to win me an election by murdering my opponent's son?" Locke's voice had grown colder, more formal, just like Holliday's when Senator Ross's guy had attacked his conscience. Fake outrage sounded like bluster, Erin thought. The real thing was usually quieter, more intense, and much more dangerous.

"You would have never known about it!" Wilburn said.

"How could you think that would make it all right?" Locke demanded.

"You don't know half the dirty tricks that get played!" Wilburn said. "For you! For everyone! That's what the game is! That's how it's done! And you don't want to know. You think your hands are clean?"

"This isn't a game," Locke said. "A young man is dead, Steve."

"People die!" Wilburn snapped. "You think Ross cares about the homeless bums who freeze to death because they can't afford jobs or shelter? You think he cares about the children who die because he won't support stronger gun control? You think—"

"How dare you!"

Locke's voice was quiet, but it had an edge to it that cut right through her campaign manager's protests. Wilburn spluttered for a moment and then he, too, fell silent.

"Steve Wilburn," Webb said, fishing his cuffs out of his hip pocket. "You're under arrest for the kidnapping and murder of Martin Ross, and the kidnapping and attempted murder of Tamara Cartwright. You have the right—"

"Look out!" Vic shouted.

None of them had thought the pudgy campaign manager had any real fight in him, and all three cops were a little slow. Vic had been the one most primed for trouble, but even he wasn't quick enough. By the time his Sig-Sauer cleared its holster, Wilburn had grabbed Madeline Locke in one hand and a dinner fork off the refreshment table in the other. The fork was shoved up under her chin, tines dimpling the skin just over her carotid.

Erin snatched out her Glock and aimed. "Drop it!" she shouted. "It's over, Wilburn!" Webb drew his own revolver.

"No way," Wilburn said. "I'm not going down for this. Not when everybody gets away with this bullshit, every day. Stay back!"

Erin was aware of movement beside her. She saw a pair of big guys, Locke's security detail, closing in. One had a Taser drawn, the other was holding an extendable baton.

"Take it easy, guys," she said, not wanting rent-a-cops to mess things up by trying to help. "We've got this. Put down the weapon, Wilburn! There's nowhere to run!"

"There's always a place to run," Wilburn said. He was steering Locke across the room, keeping her between him and the police. The staffers and volunteers parted around him like water, their faces pale with shock.

"Drop the fork," Vic said. "Or I'm gonna blow your brains out."

"Think about what you're doing, Mr. Wilburn," Webb said. "You can still plead to manslaughter on Martin Ross. You'll do some time, but you'll get out. Do anything more, and I swear you'll never see daylight except in the prison exercise yard."

"Steve," Locke said. "You did all this for me, you said. Now who are you doing it for?"

"Everyone works for themselves," Wilburn said through gritted teeth. He backed toward the elevator, step by step. "That's capitalism. It's what makes this country great."

The detectives and bodyguards followed, about ten feet away. Erin and Vic glanced at one another and, without needing to say anything, started drifting to either side, widening the angle to open a clear shot for one of them. A fork wasn't the world's deadliest weapon, but Erin knew if Wilburn drove it into Locke's carotid artery, the woman might bleed out before they could get an ambulance.

"You're not getting out of this building," Erin promised. "The only way you're leaving is in cuffs or on a gurney. Your choice."

"You must think I'm an idiot," Wilburn said. Then, to Locke, "Push the down button."

"You won't get away with this," Locke said. But she pushed the button.

"Why not?" he retorted. "People get away with shit all the time."

The doors slid open. Wilburn backed into the elevator. Vic's finger slid inside the trigger guard of his pistol. He was aiming for a headshot. Maybe, if he made a clean enough hit, Wilburn would die before he could stab Locke.

"Steady," Webb said. "Hold your fire. We'll get him. No one needs to get hurt."

The elevator doors closed.

"Parking garage," Erin said over her shoulder. She was already running for the stairs, flinging the door open. Vic was right on her heels.

"I'll cover the lobby," Webb called after them. He was staying behind with the security guys to summon the other elevator. Erin hoped and assumed he'd also be calling for backup.

"Tenth goddamn floor," Vic said through clenched teeth as they hurtled downward, grabbing the railing, taking the steps three at a time.

That meant eleven flights of stairs to reach the basement, Erin thought grimly. She didn't think she could outrun a Manhattan office elevator, but she meant to try. She went recklessly, practically leaping downward, praying silently not to miss her footing. If she put a foot wrong, it could easily mean a broken leg. Maybe she and Rolf could convalesce together.

Maybe they made plastic cones for humans, too. The dark humor made her smile on the inside.

Like most high-rises, this building had a low metal gate across the stairwell on the ground-floor landing. Most people didn't know this was to help them get out on the correct floor in the event of an evacuation. If there was smoke in the stairs, otherwise some poor schmucks might just keep going and trap themselves underground. Erin saw it coming, snatched at the rail, flexed, and jumped.

She cleared the gate and came down, felt a split second of breathless panic as her foot skidded, then her shoe's tread gripped the step and she was still moving. She heard Vic grunt behind her as he tried the same maneuver. There was no crash of a falling body, so she assumed he'd made it.

The door to the parking garage was in front of her. She slowed her dash just enough so she didn't pancake into the steel. She got her free hand on the door handle and yanked it open, sliding through just ahead of Vic.

The elevator was to their right. Erin, to her own surprise, saw the doors in the process of sliding apart. She launched herself forward, lungs screaming for air, legs aching.

Steve Wilburn still had an arm around Madeline Locke, his other hand holding the fork to her neck. He was looking the wrong direction, into the dim concrete depths of the garage, probably thinking about his car and how he was going to get away. But Locke caught Erin's movement out of the corner of her eye.

You could never tell how a civilian would react in a survival situation. Half of them would just freeze, no use to anybody. The other half would do something, and it could be almost literally anything, from panicking and grabbing at the police who were trying, to protect them, to running away, to busting out some half-remembered move they'd seen in an action movie somewhere.

Locke didn't panic and she didn't freeze. Looking Erin straight in the eye, she raised both her hands and grabbed Wilburn's right wrist, the one holding the fork.

Locke might be cool under pressure, but she was an older woman, half Wilburn's weight and no match for him in a contest of strength. However, she could keep his hand from moving for a second or two, and that was what Erin needed.

With no time to holster her Glock, Erin dropped the gun and leaped. She got Wilburn with a flying tackle. All three of them, murderer, hostage, and detective, went down in a chaos of flailing limbs. Erin felt a hard jab against her ribs and hissed in pain. She had a clear shot at Wilburn's neck and wanted nothing more than to wrap an arm around it and squeeze until she choked him out. But chokeholds were an absolute no-no in the NYPD, and had been for thirty years. However well-intentioned, that ruling limited Erin's options. She got a grip on his weapon hand and started twisting, trying to wrench the fork loose.

Wilburn headbutted her. She saw his bald pate coming at her face and lowered her own head just in time. Their foreheads connected with a loud smack. A fireworks display exploded in Erin's field of vision. The impact was almost too hard to hurt. Reeling, she somehow remembered that she needed to hold on to the hand she was holding, so she did. She pulled and twisted even harder. Somebody screamed.

"Knock it off, asshole," Vic growled. To Erin's surprise, the man who had been struggling with her went suddenly limp and very heavy. She was half under him, holding on stubbornly.

Her vision cleared and she saw Vic standing over her, holding a nasty-looking knife against Wilburn's throat and grinning. "You can let go of him now," he said. "I swear, Erin, you get more like your dog every bust we make. Next time you're gonna bite the perp."

"Detective?" Locke said in a muffled voice. "Would you mind moving your elbow?"

"Sorry," Erin gasped, shifting position. Locke was able to crawl out from under the pile of bodies while Vic slapped the cuffs on Wilburn.

Erin rolled Wilburn over onto his belly and checked his hands.

"What're you looking for?" Vic asked.

"The fork," she said.

He laughed and pointed. Erin followed his finger and saw the piece of silverware dangling from her blouse. Wilburn had driven its tines clean through the fabric just under her left breast.

"Should've worn my vest," she muttered. "That'll leave a mark. And I need a new shirt."

Locke was rearranging her disheveled clothing, straightening her skirt. "Thank you, Detectives," she said. "I don't know what would have happened without you. How did you get down here so quickly?"

"Stairs," Erin said. She was still out of breath, and the big gulps of air she was taking in were making her ribs hurt where Wilburn had jabbed her.

"Drop the fork," Vic chuckled. "Can you believe I actually said that? And what'd I tell you, Erin? A knife's a handy thing to have."

"It's not strict department policy," Erin said, timing her words to coincide with her breaths. "But close enough for government work. Steve Wilburn, you're under arrest for murder, attempted murder, kidnapping, assault with a deadly weapon..."

"'Deadly' is pushing it a little," Vic observed.

She ignored him. "You have the right to remain silent," she went on.

Wilburn just glared.

"We're going to need a statement," she said to Locke.

"Yes, of course," Locke said. "I still can't believe Steve would do something like this. I never thought he'd be capable of murder."

"You'd be surprised what people are capable of," Erin said.

Chapter 17

"This is a disaster," Madeline Locke said, perfectly calmly.

They were back at Precinct 8, in the Major Crimes office. Locke sat, somewhat gingerly, on the disreputable couch in the break room. Vic, Webb, and Erin stood around her. All of them were holding cups of coffee. Locke's security guys were outside, making up for their boss having been held hostage by glaring fiercely at anybody who happened by, whether they were in uniform or not.

"We took Mr. Wilburn into custody without anyone getting killed," Webb said. "And we have his confession."

"And you didn't get stabbed in the neck," Vic added. "That's always a plus."

"My campaign manager murdered my opponent's son," Locke said. "In the middle of a close race. This was a political assassination. I'll have to drop out of the race."

"You didn't have anything to do with it," Erin said.

Locke gave her a sad, knowing smile. "Do you really think that matters? The headlines tomorrow morning aren't going to say 'Steven Wilburn Accidentally Kills Martin Ross.' They'll say

'Locke Campaign Manager Murders Senator's Son, Locke Denies Knowledge of Actions.'"

"He threatened to kill you," Erin said. "You're a victim too."

Locke shook her head. "That won't matter either. In my line of work, Detective, if you don't get out in front of the story, the story gets in front of you. And once it's out there, you can only spin it so much. Steve wanted to help me win, but what he ended up doing has destroyed my campaign. Along with poor Martin's life, of course. I'll be drafting a personal letter to his father. Martin Ross is a bad Senator, but he's an experienced one. New York will just have to make do with the devil it knows. And then there's the young woman who was involved. Tamara, did you say?"

"Tammy Cartwright," Erin confirmed.

"Is she going to be all right?"

"She should be fine. She wasn't badly hurt."

"And the drugs?"

Erin was surprised and a little touched. "She'll be able to get treatment. Hopefully there won't be an addiction problem, but if there is, help is available."

Locke nodded. "You have my statement," she said. "Please let my office know if there's anything else you need. I hope you aren't badly hurt either, Detective."

"It's part of the Job," Erin said. She tried to act casual, but her head was throbbing and her rib cage ached.

"She could've just shot him," Vic said. "Hell, maybe she should've."

"You could've done the same," Erin said. "And you didn't."

"You know me," he said. "I hate paperwork. Fire a shot on duty and there's reams of the stuff. Hit anybody with that shot and it doubles. I got too many Fives to fill out as it is."

"That reminds me," Erin said, giving him a wicked smile. "Since you incapacitated Wilburn, technically, it's your collar. That means you get to fill out the arrest report."

"Nah, you had him fine," Vic said. "You already had your hands on him. I was just assisting. This one's all you."

Locke smiled more broadly and stood up. "Red tape exists at all levels of government," she said. "Thank you again, all of you. If there's ever anything I can do, as a private citizen of New York, I hope you won't hesitate to ask."

She shook hands all around, then left. The squad watched her go. Once she and her security detail had disappeared down the stairs, Vic shook his head.

"She looks like my third-grade math teacher, but I still like her better than Ross. It ain't right, her having to drop out of the race."

"That's outside our jurisdiction," Webb said. "You caught the killer. That was your job. O'Reilly, are you sure you don't want to get your head looked at?"

Vic guffawed. "I wonder that every day."

Erin gave him a look. "I'm fine, sir. Just a hard knock. And the fork didn't even break the skin."

"Every time you tell me you're fine, I find it a little harder to believe," Webb said dryly.

"I'm still here, aren't I?" she retorted.

"Yes, you are," he said. "Once you finish helping Neshenko write up the arrest, why don't you go home? If you won't go to the hospital to check for a concussion, that is. I won't have one of my detectives passing out or throwing up in the office."

"Nah, she can do both of those at home," Vic said. "She lives over a bar now, remember?"

"I know," Webb said, giving Erin an odd look. He hadn't said a single word to her about her relationship with Carlyle since Lieutenant Keane and Captain Holliday had cleared her.

Erin wondered just what he thought about it. Vic had figured the undercover operation out on his own, without being told, and Webb was sharper than Vic. How much did he know or guess?

"I don't need any special treatment, sir," she said. "I'll finish out my shift. If I'm going home for medical reasons, it's because I'm bleeding."

She saw Vic open his mouth to make an off-color crack about women, probably about monthly cycles. She cut him short with an upraised hand.

"Don't," she warned.

"Nobody said nothin,'" Vic said.

They finished processing the paperwork and spent the rest of the shift talking to CSU about evidence and making sure everything was properly catalogued. Wilburn himself was at Bellevue Hospital, handcuffed to a hospital bed and under guard. Vic had given him a good knock on the head, but there hadn't been any intra-cranial bleeding, so he'd probably make a full recovery. Not that it would do him much good, given the laundry list of felony charges facing him.

"You heading home?" Erin asked Vic as they shut down their computers.

"Yeah. I got big plans."

"A bottle of vodka and HBO?"

"Lucky guess."

"Why don't you come by the Corner? I'll get you a good Irish whiskey instead."

He stared at her. "I don't think that's a good idea."

"Why not?"

"I'll get in a bar fight."

"I don't think you want to fight some of those guys," she said.

"Those are exactly the guys I do want to fight," he said. Then he lowered his voice. "Besides, don't you think it might damage your cred with these lowlifes?"

"They know I hang out with cops, Vic," she said. "Since they know I'm a cop. Besides, I'm not the only Irish cop who goes there. Come on. I've got to teach you to like Glen D."

"Okay," he sighed. "But if somebody busts a bottle over my head, I'm blaming you."

*   *   *

The Barley Corner was packed to the doors when Erin and Vic got there. A raucous crowd of blue-collar guys, and a few of their girlfriends, were enjoying the spectacle of cars driving around and around an oval track at ridiculous speeds.

"Indy 500," Vic said in Erin's ear. He had to put his head close to hers so she could hear him.

"I'd forgotten that was going on," she said. She thought driving laps was silly. Real driving happened on city streets, with multiple routes, obstacles, and cross traffic.

"I bet a lot of money changes hands in here tonight," he said.

She didn't answer, but she knew he was right. Carlyle was heavily involved with under-the-table sports betting, and the biggest car race of the year was bound to be a money-maker. She eased through the crowd toward the bar. Vic, twice as wide in the shoulders as she was, had more trouble and fell behind. He got momentarily jammed between a couple of enormous construction workers, one of whom gave him a faceful of beer breath and what was meant to be a friendly clap on the shoulder.

As she crossed the room, she heard a familiar voice from one of the side booths amid the confusion. She only caught a few of the words, but she recognized James Corcoran's Belfast brogue.

"...don't see why you'd be upset, lad," he was saying. "I'm afraid the big fella's made himself a mite unpopular with the other lads."

Erin glanced over without much interest, on the principle that it was always a good idea to know what Corky was up to. She saw him sitting opposite a large, scary-looking guy with no neck. The other guy was in the process of standing up, looming over Corky. That man looked pissed off.

She did a double take. The big guy was Detective Lacroix.

Lacroix bent over the smaller man, gripping the edge of the table. Erin saw old scars on his knuckles, the sort you got from bare-knuckle fistfights. "Do I need to tell you the shitstorm I can bring down on you?" he growled. "This isn't a negotiation."

Corky was smiling, apparently completely at ease in spite of the physical menace of the detective. "Everything's a negotiation, lad, right until the knives come out."

"What's up?" Vic asked over Erin's shoulder.

In answer, she cocked her head toward the booth. They were standing just close enough to hear the conversation, but neither man in the booth had noticed them.

"You can deliver the Teamsters," Lacroix said. "And you're going to, if you know what's good for you."

Corky was still smiling. "It was the carrot before. Now you're the stick, if I'm reading you right. Carrot or stick, though, it's not changing the situation. My lads think Mrs. Locke's got their interests more to heart than Ross does. Have you ever tried changing an Irishman's mind, when once it's made up?"

"Make it happen, pipsqueak," Lacroix growled. "My guy's not happy with you, and if you don't watch it, I'll put you the hell out of business."

"Now that's a thing I'd like to see," Corky said. "Millions of people in this fine city, going about their business, and thousands of truckers bringing their food and carrying out their litter, and you're going to shut it down? Lad, if you're going to make threats, it's better to make them believable."

"How about this one?" Lacroix replied. "Give Ross that endorsement, or you can watch the results on election night on a hospital TV while you're lying in traction."

"That's better," Corky said. "It's good to know you're teachable. Now, if you'll excuse me, I've some obligations to attend to." He started to rise.

Lacroix planted his meaty palm in the middle of Corky's chest and shoved him back into his seat. "What's your answer?" he demanded. "And don't think about pulling one of your famous knives on me. I'm a police detective, remember?"

Erin was watching in astonishment, genuinely unsure whether to believe what she was seeing. An NYPD detective threatening a man in the middle of a busy pub in downtown Manhattan? She knew she ought to do something, but wasn't immediately sure what.

Vic slid past her, stealing the moment. He laid a hand on Lacroix's shoulder.

"Eddie Lacroix," he said. "I thought it was you. How long's it been since we were in ESU together? Seems like just yesterday."

Lacroix spun to face Vic, angry puzzlement written all over him. "Neshenko? What the hell are you doing here?"

Corky exchanged glances with Erin. He didn't seem at all surprised to see her, but Vic's presence apparently puzzled him. He raised an eyebrow. She shrugged her shoulders slightly.

"Oh, you know me," Vic said. "Just keeping the streets safe. But I'm sorry, I'm interrupting something. You were just telling this lowlife what you were gonna do to him if he didn't vote for your guy, or something like that."

"Not your problem, Neshenko," Lacroix said. "We're just sorting out a little political misunderstanding."

"Tell you the truth, I don't really care about politics," Vic said. "Makes my head hurt. And I love wearing a shield. But you know what I really hate?"

"What's that?"

"Scumbags who hide behind their shield." Then Vic punched Lacroix in the face.

It was a serious punch, with all the Russian's considerable weight and muscle behind it. Lacroix was a big guy, but the impact drove him right off his feet. He slid across Corky's table into the wall, spilling Corky's half-empty beer and sending the mug clattering toward the floor. Corky caught it halfway.

"Lad," Corky began.

"Relax," Vic said. "I'll buy you another." He turned to Erin with a grin. "It was worth it."

Erin, looking over Vic's shoulder, saw Lacroix come back up, blood streaming from his nose. She couldn't believe a man could get up so fast from a hit like that. Her eyes went wide.

Vic saw the change in her expression and started to turn back to face his opponent. Lacroix's fist caught him on the upper part of his chest and spun him halfway around. The sound was like a butcher's cleaver chopping into a big chunk of meat.

"You like that?" Lacroix snarled. "Sucker-punch me, you son of a bitch?" He hit Vic again, center mass, and again, using his fists like hammers.

Vic grunted but didn't go down. He blocked the third punch with his forearm and countered with a left jab into Lacroix's stomach. A space was clearing around the booth as the Corner's other patrons got out of the way, forming a circle.

"Knock it off!" Erin shouted, but nobody was listening to her. If this had been anybody else, she'd have jumped right in on Vic's side, but he was fighting another cop, for God's sake, and he'd thrown the first punch. Who should she arrest?

While she hesitated, the two men traded punches. Vic was taller than Lacroix, but the Homicide detective was every bit as heavily muscled, and both men were clearly no strangers to the world of boxing. Now that the advantage of surprise was gone, they parried and deflected the blows each aimed at the other's head.

Erin saw an enormous shape moving through the crowd toward the fight. Mickey Connor, head and shoulders above everyone around him, was wading their way. Ian was probably coming, too, or whatever other security guys Carlyle had on duty. This was getting out of hand. This fight needed to end soon, before it turned into a free-for-all and someone really got hurt.

Vic launched a vicious three-punch combo, left-right-left, ending with a short, hard uppercut that sent Lacroix reeling back against a table. The Russian followed it up with a haymaker intended to flatten the guy.

Lacroix grabbed a chair, recently vacated, and smashed it into Vic's side. Vic stumbled and his swing went wide. Lacroix pulled the chair back for another blow. Vic, off-balance, took a wild swing. It connected and it was Lacroix's turn to spin as he took the hit high on the cheek.

Glass shattered. Lacroix blinked. Then his legs turned to rubber and he collapsed to the floor.

Corky shrugged almost apologetically. He was holding the handle of his beer mug, all that was left of it. "Sorry, lad," he said to Vic. "Not meaning to cut into your fun, but once that scunner picked up a weapon, I reckoned the fight was a bit less private than before." He grinned. "Besides, you did promise to buy me a drink, and it'd be hard to redeem that offer with a broken head."

Erin knelt beside Lacroix and checked his pulse. To her relief, it was rapid, but healthy. "He'll live," she said to no one in particular.

"What's goin' on here?" Mickey demanded, forcing his way through.

"Police business," Vic said, holding up his shield.

He and Mickey looked one another up and down. Mickey looked at Vic, then at Erin and Corky and the unconscious Lacroix. He snorted. "Bunch of pencil-dicks," he said.

"Everything okay, ma'am?"

Erin jumped. Ian had somehow managed to come up right alongside her without being noticed. She figured she'd been distracted by the fight and by Mickey.

"No trouble," she said. "Vic and Lacroix, here, are old acquaintances."

"Expecting any blowback?" Ian asked.

"Forget about it," she said. "They're both cops. We'll handle it."

He nodded. "Roger that. We better get him out of here."

The crowd was losing interest, now that the fight was over. They turned back to the car race on the TV screens. Mickey lingered a moment, but finally shambled off, to Erin's relief.

"I'll take the shoulders," Vic said. "You wanna get his legs?"

They carried Lacroix out onto the pavement. By the time they got him outside, he was already coming around. Unconsciousness didn't usually last very long, whatever the movies said.

"You good?" Vic asked. He deftly drew Lacroix's gun, ejected the magazine, racked the slide, and returned the empty pistol to its holster. It was never wise to leave a loaded weapon in the hands of a man you'd just cold-cocked.

Lacroix groaned and put a hand to his head.

"Might wanna get that checked out," Vic advised. "And take some advice. Next time you get the urge to play gangster, don't."

*   *   *

"You could've arrested him," Erin said.

"Really?" Vic looked surprised. "You think anybody wants that?" They watched Lacroix's car pull away, driven by a sore but reasonably alert Homicide detective.

"I can't even imagine what Keane would say," she said.

He gingerly prodded a swelling under his eye. "It's better to keep IAB out of this," he said. "Besides, Lacroix always was a punk. I just can't believe I slugged a cop to protect a mobster."

"Welcome to my world," Erin said, giving him a lopsided smile. "But you could get in some trouble for this."

"What's he gonna do?" Vic retorted. "Make an official report about how he was shaking down a guy and I got in the way? You think I give a damn about his political connections? Now, you gonna get me that whiskey, or what?"

Corky was at the bar next to Carlyle when they got back inside. Both men stood up to greet the detectives.

"Corky's been telling me what happened," Carlyle said to Erin. "It seems your mate here assisted mine, and for that I'm grateful." He offered Vic his hand. Vic pretended not to see it.

"Aye, Cars and I have been talking it over," Corky said. "And I'll have to decline your generous offer. I'll be doing the buying. What'll you have?"

"Erin says the Glen D's pretty good," Vic said.

"Then that's what you'll be drinking," Corky said. "Excellent choice. Comes from a wee little town in Scotland. What's the name of it again?"

"Glen Docherty-Kinlochewe," Carlyle said.

"I believe they've been making the stuff there for the past thousand years or so," Corky said. "You've not lived till you've tried their thirty-year Scotch."

"What was that all about, anyway?" Erin asked. "I know you had a meeting with Senator Ross."

"Ah, just the usual garden-variety political corruption," Corky said cheerfully. "He wanted to purchase the Teamsters' endorsement for his campaign. I had to decline."

"That seems uncharacteristic," she said.

"Are you implying I'm for sale to the highest bidder?" he asked with a pained expression. "I may be easy at times, love, but I don't hold myself cheap."

"So the Teamsters are endorsing Locke?"

He nodded. "She's a friend of the working man."

"Ross shouldn't have bothered," she said gloomily. "Locke's about to drop out of the race."

"She never!" Corky exclaimed. "Why?"

Vic sampled the whiskey Danny put in front of him. "This is damn good," was his considered opinion.

"Better than vodka?" Erin asked.

"I wouldn't go quite that far."

"You're evading my question, love," Corky said.

"Aye," Erin said, mimicking his accent. "Now where do you think I learned to do that?"

Corky and Carlyle both laughed.

"You can read about it in tomorrow's paper," she said. "Where's Rolf?"

"Upstairs," Carlyle said. "He's been moping about on my couch all day, I fear. Poor lad, I imagine he thinks he's done something terrible. I've seen lads just out of jail with the same sorry, hang-dog look."

"I'd better go see him," she said.

"I'll come with you," Carlyle offered.

"And I'll stay here, drinking your liquor," Corky said. "With my new mate. What's your name, lad?"

"Vic," Vic said. "We've met."

"Aye, but that was in the course of business, and we were never properly introduced. Now that we're drinking together, we'd best be on a first-name basis. Corky Corcoran, at your service."

"That's not your first name," Erin pointed out.

"A nickname's even better," he said. "I'd never ask any of you to call me James. Only the penguins called me that."

"Penguins?" Vic echoed.

"We went to Catholic school," Carlyle explained. "That's what Corky always called the nuns."

On their way upstairs, Erin shook her head. "I can't believe Vic and Corky are sharing a drink."

"They fought side by side," Carlyle said. "An experience like that brings lads closer. Not to fear, they'll be hating one another again come morning, once the adrenaline wears off."

"And the alcohol," she added.

"That, too."

"Vic was right, though. He predicted he'd get in a bar fight."

"Now that's a self-fulfilling prophecy if I've ever heard one," Carlyle said.

Chapter 18

One of the many reasons Erin liked dogs better than people was that they didn't hold grudges. The moment he saw her, Rolf was up off the couch, tail wagging so hard his whole back half was moving. He came running and limping to meet her, caught the edge of his cone on the doorway, and lurched sideways. The K-9 shook his head in confusion, recovered, and kept coming. Erin dropped to one knee in front of him and took hold of his head behind the ears. She'd have to get him a better cone, one of those plush Velcro jobs.

"I'm sorry," she said, kissing his forehead. "It's okay. You'll be back soon, I promise."

Rolf kept wagging. He was ready now. There were bad guys to chase, he just knew it.

Carlyle laughed. "He and I are kindred spirits these days," he said. "Two lads lying about, licking our wounds and feeling sorry for ourselves."

"I'd better take him out," Erin said. "Give him a little exercise. And I can make sure Corky and Vic aren't killing each other yet."

She leashed Rolf and took him downstairs. The Shepherd was limping but trying not to show any pain. He'd pretend a bullet didn't hurt if he got shot, Erin thought. Being left at home hurt him more than any weapon could. Right then, she made her decision.

"You're coming back to work with me," she said to him. "Limited duty. I'm not letting you chase perps, and you have to stay calm. That's the deal. Understand?"

Rolf looked up at her with pure devotion. He understood he'd be coming with her. The rest was irrelevant details.

They found Vic and Corky at the bar, already on their second round. Vic was telling how he'd cold-cocked Steve Wilburn.

"Then you've no objection to how I ended your wee scrap," Corky said. "So that's why the charming Madeline is leaving the race?"

"That's about it," Erin agreed, joining them and signaling Danny to bring her a drink.

"Oh, that's nonsense," Corky said cheerfully. "Murder's not what brings down the big ones."

"Really?" Erin said.

"Of course not. Wasn't it Ben Franklin who said the only certainties were death and taxes?"

"Yeah," Vic said.

"The government's better at handling taxes than death," Corky said. "They don't care if you die, but you've got to pay. Financial misconduct is what trips up lads like Capone. And Ross. Mark my words, he'll be looking worse than Locke come this time tomorrow."

"What do you know?" Erin asked sharply.

Corky just smiled and clinked his glass against hers. "More than yourself, love, at times."

"I dunno about that," Vic said. "I know some shit, too."

"Such as?" Corky inquired.

"You're gonna die on the street or in prison, probably soon," Vic said.

Corky grinned. "Oh, lad, I've known that for years. The Life's a young lad's game, and I'm out of warranty. I'll just drive until my wheels fall off."

"I'm taking Rolf out to stretch his legs," Erin said.

"I think I'll shove off," Vic said. "I've had my drink and my fight. No need to hang around."

"I hope to see more of you, big fella," Corky said.

Vic grunted and departed.

"You've got something on Ross," Erin said. "You plan on taking him down?"

Corky just smiled.

"Why?" she asked. "What's in it for you?"

"I've told you," he said. "He's no friend to the Teamsters. We'll do better with Locke. Besides, sending his lad to threaten me wasn't polite. If I didn't return the favor, what sort of lad would I be?"

* * *

"This isn't a pet hospital," Webb said when Erin and Rolf walked into Major Crimes the next morning.

Rolf, wearing a new soft cone, ignored the Lieutenant and settled in his customary spot next to Erin's desk.

"He'll be fine," Erin said.

"Did you see the news?" Webb asked.

"Not yet. What's up?"

In answer, Webb handed her a copy of the Times. The front page was all politics, but the top headline wasn't what she'd expected. LOCKE TAKEN HOSTAGE BY OWN CAMPAIGN MANAGER, RESCUED BY NYPD was actually the second story, under the fold. The lead read, SENATOR ROSS IMPLICATED IN BRIBERY, COERCION.

Erin scanned the story, which detailed three anonymous sources' reports that Marcus Ross and his representatives had attempted to purchase influence with the Teamsters Union, along with several other prominent labor unions. Some of these unions' representatives, their sense of civic duty inflamed, had leaked details of the meetings. Nowhere was there any mention of Madeline Locke dropping out of the race. The Ross campaign had issued a terse statement that there was no truth to the allegations, but that Marcus Ross was retiring from politics for personal reasons related to the sudden death of his only child. He would serve out the rest of his term, but would no longer seek reelection.

"That got messy fast," Erin observed.

"Just be glad it's not our mess," Webb said. "By the way, Neshenko was in just before you, and he got called up to Keane's office. Any idea what that's about?"

"The Bloodhound wanted to talk to Vic?" Erin asked, trying to look surprised. "Did Vic say anything?"

"No, but he'd been in a fight," Webb said. "He's got a big bruise on his face and Band-Aids on his knuckles."

"He could've picked up those bumps taking down Wilburn," Erin said.

"But he didn't," Webb said, giving her a sharp glance. "The arrest report said you were the one who was up close with him. Neshenko just pistol-whipped him from behind."

"It happened pretty fast," Erin said lamely, cursing inwardly. It was easy to forget what a good detective Webb was.

"I'm not asking you to rat out your partner," Webb said. "Just tell me if you think any of this is going to come back on us."

"I don't think so, sir."

Erin got a cup of coffee and settled herself in for a boring morning catching up on paperwork and departmental communications. Vic came downstairs from his meeting with Internal Affairs with an expression on his face like he'd been chewing lemons.

"Still got a job?" she asked.

"And a pension, if I can stand it long enough," he said.

"Well?" Webb asked.

"Well what?" Vic replied.

"What did Keane want?"

"Somebody told him I'd been mixing it up with some Homicide dick after hours in a bar."

"What did you tell him?" Webb asked.

"I told him that'd be a crazy thing to do," Vic said. "And I asked if he'd talked to this Homicide guy, whoever he was. He just smiled that goddamn smile of his and told me to have a good day. It's creepy when IAB tells you that."

"Well, I'm glad it was nothing," Webb said. But Erin saw the way he looked at Vic. He knew. So did Keane. Keane wanted Vic to know he knew. That was the way Keane was. He'd move on it in his own good time, for his own reasons, or not. And in the meantime, Vic would have to sweat.

Not that Vic would. He'd shrug and move on. It was liberating not to care about promotions or the future. Erin wished she could let go of things that easily.

"I heard from Piekarski," Vic said, changing the subject. "They knocked down the charges on most of those mopes from the pizza joint. Piddling little misdemeanors. They're gonna do probation or community service or some crap like that. We've still got the jerk who shot Firelli. He's gonna do hard time. They transferred him to Riker's first thing this morning."

Erin nodded. "Price of doing business," she said.

"I still don't like it," he said.

"You don't have to like it," Webb said. "But it worked. We got the murderer, thanks to that tip. That's how this works, Neshenko. O'Reilly gets that, which may be why she's a Detective Second Grade and you'll be at the bottom of the ladder for the foreseeable future. Probably forever."

"Thanks, Dad," Vic said sourly.

"You mean, 'thank you, sir,'" Webb corrected him.

"Thank you, sir, for reminding me of the proper etiquette in the New York Police Department, sir," Vic said. "It's an honor, sir, to come to this office and sit within line of sight of your impressive and leader-like image, sir. It's more than this poor Detective Third Grade deserves, sir."

Erin stifled a snicker.

Vic's phone buzzed. He fished it out. "Hey," he said in a more pleasant tone of voice, which Erin took to mean he was talking either to Piekarski, or maybe his mom. "We just talked. Everything okay?"

As he listened, his expression slid back into sourness by way of surprise. "Really," he said flatly. "Okay, thanks. No, you're right. The bastard had it coming. Thanks for the heads-up."

"What happened?" Erin asked after he'd hung up.

"They just processed our shooter at Riker's," Vic said. "No need to segregate him, right? I mean, he took a shot at a cop. That ought to make him popular in there. So they dumped him into GenPop. He hadn't been there ten minutes when some lifer shanked him with a sharpened toothbrush handle."

"What's his prognosis?" Webb asked.

Vic snorted. "You kidding? He's dead. The guy who stabbed him was some old-school Mafia boy who's doing something like five life sentences. Paolo Napoli."

"Who's this Napoli affiliated with?" Webb asked. "One of the other Mafia families?"

Erin shook her head. She already suspected the answer, but she called up Napoli's jacket on her computer. "Paolo 'the Throat,' Napoli," she read aloud. "He's a made man with the Lucarellis, a personal friend of Old Man Acerbo."

"Why's he called that?" Webb asked.

"His MO," she said. "He likes to cut throats. Apparently his deal was to come up from behind and cut right to the backbone. He's got five murder convictions." She paused. "I guess this'll make six."

"Why'd a Lucarelli off this jerk?" Vic asked. "I mean, it makes no difference to Napoli. He's never getting out, and we don't execute people anymore. I swear, they oughta dust off the electric chair just for guys like this."

"You're mad because one mobster killed another?" Webb asked.

"Hell, no. It'll save the state some money. I'm mad because once a guy goes that bad, he can just keep doing shit, because he's already gotten as much as we can throw at him. He's a damn sociopath, so it's not like throwing him in Solitary will make him change his ways."

"Vinnie had this done," Erin said quietly. "It's not the first time he's killed his own guys."

"Right, the Bianchi thing," Webb said. "I remember. It's one hell of a way to keep his house in order."

"He offered to take care of this for us," she said. "I guess, in a way, he thought he was honoring his end of the bargain."

"Honor," Vic snorted. "How's it honorable to stab a guy with a damn toothbrush?"

"I guess you'll never be a Mafioso, either," Webb said. "Your career options are sadly limited."

"Thank God for small favors," Vic muttered. "At least this way I don't have to worry about being stabbed by guys I thought were my buddies."

Erin nodded, but her thoughts were elsewhere. She got up from her desk and went into the break room. Once she was sure no one was listening, she took out her special burner phone and called her contact "Leo."

"Can you talk?" he said.

"Yeah, I'm clean," she said. "But we need to have a conversation, face to face. Can we meet sometime today?"

"Sure. Can you make it to Duarte Square, off Canal Street, at noon?"

"Copy that. I'll be there."

*   *   *

Erin circled the block twice to make sure she wasn't being followed, then parked in a police spot next to Duarte Square. It was a pleasant strip of small trees and benches, just the sort of place for a casual meeting. She spotted her contact immediately.

Phil Stachowski was sitting on a bench, newspaper in hand, looking more like an out-of-work professor than what he was, which was an NYPD Lieutenant with a specialty in undercover assignments. He was a pleasant, mild guy in a tweed jacket and spectacles. His hairline was receding at about the same pace as his waistline was expanding. If he carried a gun, Erin couldn't see it on him.

For all his harmless appearance, his street senses were razor sharp. He'd made her before she'd seen him. He nodded a greeting when she approached. She slid onto the bench next to him.

"Hi, Erin," he said. "Everything okay? Looks like your partner got the short end of it."

Rolf settled on his haunches beside the bench and pretended he was completely intact, cone and all.

"He'll be fine," she said. "Just gashed his paw on some broken glass chasing down a mope."

"You get your man?"

"Of course he did. It takes more than a little cut to stop this bad boy." She reached into the cone and scratched Rolf behind the ears.

"How're you holding up?" he asked.

She shrugged. "I'm fine. Everybody knows me at the Corner now. They expect me. I did that favor for Veronica that we talked about, got her girls sprung. That should play well with Evan."

Erin paused and looked around the park. She knew what she was going to say, but for once, she was reluctant to bring it up.

Phil let her take her time, sitting next to her in companionable silence. The sun was warm on her face and hands. The square was an island of serenity in the middle of Manhattan's constant bustle.

"I'm going to need that wire," she said finally.

He nodded, unsurprised. "You sure?"

"Yeah. I should've already had it on me. I could've implicated Vincenzo Moreno."

"Vinnie the Oil Man?" Phil was surprised. "What's he got to do with the O'Malleys?"

"Nothing. At least, nothing I know of. They hate each other. You know Vinnie?"

"I know of him. He's a smooth operator, by all accounts. How did he get clumsy enough to spill something to you?"

She smiled grimly. "I've got a street rep now, didn't you know? I'm a cop they can do business with. We swept up a bunch of Vinnie's guys in a drug bust. Got some guns, too, and one of the idiots shot one of our guys."

"That thing with SNEU in Little Italy? Yeah, I heard about that."

"You're well-informed."

It was his turn to smile. "It pays to know what's happening streetside. I keep my ear to the pavement and I've got a couple guys who know what's going on with the Lucarellis. So Vinnie came to you with an offer?"

"Yeah. He cracked our murder. All I had to do was get his boys off the hook."

"You sprang a guy who shot one of ours?"

She shook her head. "Nope. The rest of them. Vinnie took care of the shooter."

"You mean..."

"Yeah. In Riker's, right after the bastard arrived."

Phil blinked. "I see. Did he tell you that was going to happen?"

"Not in so many words. But he implied it. One of his guys, a lifer, took out the shooter with a prison shiv. Vinnie must've passed the order along."

"I can see why you'd want a record of that conversation," Phil said. He whistled softly. "Well, congratulations, Erin. You're definitely on the inside. I'll get the equipment for you and we'll go through how to set it up. Don't worry, this isn't like the old days. It used to be you'd have a whole tape deck crammed down the back of your trousers and a big black wire clipped to your shirt. And half the time those things would malfunction. No, we've got miniature mics we can sew right into your clothes. They're not likely to find them unless they make a real search, right down to the skin."

Erin nodded. "I can handle it."

He looked closely at her. "It's not the hardware that gives people away when they blow their cover," he said. "It's knowing you're wearing it. You've got to be careful how you talk. Be natural. Don't ask leading questions. Don't be stiff, and don't play to the microphone. Believe me, these guys will notice things like that. The best thing to do is convince yourself it's not turned on. Forget you're wearing it. Then you'll be able to relax."

She laughed quietly. "As much as I ever can around these guys. How long is this operation going to run?"

"We still don't know," he said. "Your friend's gotten us some valuable information already, and he's agreed to be wired, too. The longer and deeper we can go, the better. We're going for a clean sweep, remember. And we still need Evan's ledgers. If we can track down his money, that's the ball game. Seize the assets and he goes down hard, just like Capone."

"You still don't know where he keeps his books?"

Phil shook his head. "Neither does your guy. But we're working on it. In the meantime, just do what you do best."

"Phil?"

"What is it?"

"What happens once it's over?"

He seemed surprised. "We have a trial, assuming they don't all plead guilty. They go to prison, you go back to work. Don't worry, whatever odds and ends are left after we sweep up the O'Malleys won't bother coming after you. They'll have bigger problems. Police don't usually have to worry about blowback."

"I mean, what happens to... him?"

"Oh." Phil looked down at his hands. "Erin, I don't have to tell you, because you're smart. It's really dangerous, what you're doing with him. He's a former terrorist and a career criminal. He's not going to prison. He's got an airtight immunity deal. If Evan goes down, your guy walks. But maybe you and he ought to walk in different directions."

Erin felt her jaw tighten. "Phil, he's doing this for me," she said. "He's giving up his job for me. Hell, he took a damn bullet for me! He's not playing me. And I'm not playing him."

"I didn't say that. But it's hard for a guy who's lived his whole life on the streets to go legit. Most of the guys who go into WitSec slide right back into crime again, did you know that?"

"He's not most guys," she said stubbornly. "I'm standing by him."

"Okay." Phil held up a hand in surrender. "I'm not giving you orders, Erin, just advice. Being a romantic is dangerous in our line of work."

"How would you know?" she shot back.

"Because I am one," he said. "I believe in happy endings. I believe there's a pot of gold at the end of the rainbow. It's stupid of me, I'm old enough to know better, and I try to warn people off, but there it is. Believe me, if you and he make a go of it, I'll be right there at your wedding, cheering louder than anyone. I just don't like your odds."

"Hey," Erin said. "If it was easy, what'd be the point? Besides, I'm getting used to the danger."

"It's easier to deal with the devil you know," Phil said, smiling. "But if you want the happily ever after, you've got to earn it. You ready to go back to work?"

Erin O'Reilly stood up. Rolf sprang to his feet beside her, tail wagging, ready for action.

"Let's take these bastards down," she said.

Keep reading for a sneak peek from

Hair of the Dog

The Erin O'Reilly Mysteries, Book 14

Here's a sneak peek from Book 14: Hair of the Dog

Coming 12/20/21

Sean O'Reilly would never really stop being a cop. He might be retired. He might have less hair and more gut than when he'd walked a Patrol beat in Queens. His mustache might have turned white. He might have to wear reading glasses to make sense of the morning paper. But his instincts were still razor sharp. He could take the measure of a man in an instant, recognizing potential threats or weaknesses. He always knew who was in the room with him and where they were. He liked to put his back against the wall, so no one could get behind him. And he always, always watched the other guy's hands.

He'd drilled the mantra into his daughter years before Erin O'Reilly had put on her own shield and gun: *What will hurt you? Hands will hurt you. Watch the hands.*

Now, Sean stood in the living room of his oldest son's house facing Erin and the man at her elbow. He hardly glanced at his only daughter, though she knew he loved her more than he'd ever been able to say. With his veteran policeman's eye, he'd zeroed in on her dinner date.

The two men watched one another with the wary respect reserved for a dangerous opponent. It was like a pair of chess masters squaring off before making the first move, Erin thought. Or maybe a pair of gunslingers in some dusty street in the Old West.

"Evening, Mr. O'Reilly," Morton Carlyle said in his distinctive Belfast brogue. "I'm pleased to meet you under such pleasant circumstances." He extended his hand.

Sean didn't move. He watched that hand and its mate. Both were empty, clean, with well-trimmed nails. They were the hands of a businessman, the wrists disappearing into sleeves of Italian silk. Carlyle was wearing one of his best suits, a charcoal-gray Armani accented by a burgundy necktie and pocket handkerchief.

Erin had been dreading this meeting for months. Her father and her boyfriend had successfully avoided one another as long as they could. The last time they'd met face-to-face had been almost twenty years ago, when Carlyle had been a young gangster and Sean an ordinary Patrol cop. Carlyle, with his usual conversational deftness, had reminded Sean that their previous encounter had been less pleasant, but ultimately useful. It had probably saved Sean's career by giving him the information he needed to escape a corruption scandal. Sean had distrusted and resented Carlyle ever since. Finding out his daughter had fallen in love with the mobster had not improved his view of the man.

Carlyle's hand hung in the air, an unanswered offer.

Erin fought the urge to roll her eyes. Instead, she slipped her own hand into Carlyle's left, interlacing their fingers. Her message was clear. They were a unit now, and Sean would have to accept Carlyle because Erin already had.

Sean's mustache twitched irritably. "Glad you could join us," he said, sounding anything but. However, he did take the offered hand at last, giving the other man a brisk, firm handshake.

Erin let out the breath she'd been holding. The other adults in the room also relaxed, feeling the release of tension. Erin's brother, Sean Junior, and his wife Michelle came forward. Michelle put her arms around Carlyle's shoulders and gave him a kiss on the cheek. Sean Junior offered his own hand.

"How's the stomach?" he asked.

"Grand," Carlyle said. "You did a fine job stitching me up. I'm well mended, I'm thinking. I'd be happy to give you a glowing reference."

"No, thanks. I get too much business as it is." Sean Junior was a trauma surgeon at Bellevue Hospital. "Just do me a favor and try not to stop any more bullets. I hate having to redo my work."

Michelle had moved on to the last guest in her home. "Ian!" she exclaimed. "I was hoping you'd be joining us, too. Welcome back!"

Ian Thompson, Carlyle's driver and chief bodyguard, shifted uncomfortably. He wasn't used to being greeted with such enthusiasm. But he managed the closest thing to a smile Erin had ever seen on his face and submitted to Michelle's hug and kiss. Once he'd disengaged, he made his way to the front window and kept an eye on the street, probably looking for potential hitmen.

Anna and Patrick, Erin's niece and nephew, were already engrossed in a game with Erin's partner Rolf. Anna had a tennis ball which she was trying to hide. Rolf, an expert at search-and-rescue, nosed it out wherever she put it, retrieving the ball from under the couch, behind the seat cushions, and the base of the curtains. The German Shepherd K-9 was having a great time, his tail wagging eagerly, his gigantic ears fully upright.

The dinner party had been Michelle's idea, of course. Shelley was a romantic at heart, and ever since meeting Carlyle, she'd been planning to bring him together with Erin's folks. In her view, it would help cement them as one big happy family. She didn't seem to realize just how complicated the situation was, or how awkward Erin's position in it might be.

"Where's Mom?" Erin asked.

"In the kitchen, naturally," Michelle said. "She's just putting the finishing touches on one of her famous triple-berry pies. It should be out of the oven by the time we're done with dinner."

"What's cooking?" Erin asked.

"It smells lovely," Carlyle said.

"Roast chicken with asparagus," Michelle said. "It's in a mustard cream sauce, with tarragon, garlic, and shallots. Boiled potatoes on the side."

"I don't like asparagus," Anna announced, pausing in her game. The tennis ball was poised in her hand. Rolf, transfixed by the ball, stood with one paw raised, waiting.

"When's the last time you tried it?" her mother replied.

"At Debbie Lynn's house," Anna said. "It was yucky."

"Then Debbie's mother didn't cook it properly," Michelle said.

Erin only listened to the others with half an ear. Her attention was still on her dad and Carlyle. The two men were definitely on their best behavior. Carlyle was more outwardly relaxed than Sean, but they continued to watch one another. She hoped her dad had left all his guns at home.

Carlyle was right. Dinner did smell delicious. The O'Reillys and their guests sat down around a table full of good things. Ian made a halfhearted effort to stand clear of the meal, explaining he was on duty, but Michelle was having none of it, so he was seated between Anna and Erin.

"Would you like to say grace, Mr. Carlyle?" Michelle asked.

He was startled, but covered it with a pleasant smile. "I'd be honored," he said. They all bowed their heads while the Irishman began the traditional Catholic table blessing. "Bless us, O Lord, and these, Thy gifts, which we are about to receive from Thy bounty. Through—"

Erin's phone buzzed.

"—Christ, our Lord. Amen," Carlyle finished.

"I hate those things," Mary O'Reilly said. "Our generation got on fine without them."

Erin looked at her phone's screen and sighed. "I have to take this," she said, pushing her chair back from the table and thumbing the Smartphone. "O'Reilly."

"I know you're off duty," Lieutenant Webb said. "So I'm sorry to call you. But there's a situation."

"What is it?" she asked, sudden anxiety sharpening her voice. Something was wrong. Webb didn't sound normal. Maybe an officer had been wounded, or even killed. Maybe there'd been some sort of terrorist incident. Maybe—

"How fast can you get to Long Island?" he asked.

"I'm at my brother's in Midtown," she said. "Maybe twenty or thirty minutes?"

"Make it twenty," he said. "It's a Brooklyn address. I'll text it to you."

"Sir, what's going on?"

"I caught a body," Webb said, and that was weird, too. He usually would have said "we," not "I."

"Is there a problem, sir?"

"No problem, O'Reilly. Just get here as fast as you can." And Webb hung up.

Erin looked around at the expectant, worried faces at the dinner table. "I have to go," she said lamely. "Work."

Sean nodded his understanding, as did Erin's brother. Both of them knew that the job sometimes came first, even before a meal cooked by Michelle O'Reilly, who was the family gourmet.

Erin didn't want to go. She needed to be here, chaperoning the encounter between Carlyle and her father and making sure things didn't get off on the wrong foot. But that strange note in Webb's voice nagged at her. Webb was a tough, cynical old gumshoe, and he'd sounded different. He'd sounded almost scared.

"Rolf," she said, standing up. The Shepherd sprang up instantly, awaiting instructions. "*Komm,*" she said, using the German command he'd been taught as a puppy in Bavaria.

Criminals didn't keep respectable business hours. The Job was calling, so it was time for Detective O'Reilly to go to work.

*   *   *

The address Webb sent to Erin's phone was on Marlborough Road in Prospect Park South, a small, upscale Brooklyn neighborhood. The houses tended to be fancy, with spacious porches and many sporting bay windows and round towers. It wasn't the sort of neighborhood a Major Crimes cop expected to be summoned to.

"I guess people get killed everywhere," she said to her K-9.

Rolf didn't argue. He was glad to be out with her. As far as he was concerned, chasing down bad guys was even better than lurking under Anna's chair waiting for food to get dropped.

Erin pulled up in front of what was either a large house or a small mansion, depending on context. She parked behind the familiar shape of Vic Neshenko's unmarked Taurus. The other car on the street was a slightly rusty Oldsmobile, a car about as out of place in this swanky area as a street bum at a black-tie dinner. She didn't see any officially-marked NYPD vehicles, which was strange. She also saw no sign of an ambulance or of the coroner's van. In fact, if not for Vic's car, she would have assumed she'd come to the wrong address.

"Something smells about this," she muttered, taking a moment to strap on her Kevlar vest and do a quick chamber check on her Glock, ensuring it was loaded and ready.

Rolf wagged his tail. He liked smells. Maybe they'd get out of the car soon and find something to sniff.

Erin opened her Charger's door and stepped onto the street. It was about seven o'clock. The sun was getting low in the sky, shadows stretching across the pavement. She saw a light over the door of the house, and another shining through the living room blinds. The ordinariness of the scene made her skin crawl. Something was wrong, she just didn't know what.

"*Your old man's a cop,*" her dad had once told her. "*You bleed blue, just like me. It's in your veins. If your gut tells you something, listen to it. Your insides know more than you think they do.*"

Erin unloaded Rolf from his compartment and strapped on the dog's body armor. Then she walked quickly up the sidewalk to the front door, going up the porch steps on the side instead of in the middle so they didn't creak. She paused at the door, leaning in and listening, one hand holding Rolf's leash, the other resting on the grip of her pistol.

She heard voices coming faintly through the woodwork and relaxed. She recognized Webb and Vic, along with a third voice she didn't know, a woman. No one sounded violent, or even particularly angry.

She knocked on the door. "It's me, O'Reilly," she announced loudly.

Vic Neshenko opened the door. The big Russian detective was an intimidating sight, what with his bulky six-foot-three body topped by a face with a crooked, twice-broken nose. But Erin found him comforting. He was rock solid in a fight and much smarter than he looked.

"What's the deal?" Erin asked, trying to see past him into the house. Vic tended to fill up a doorway.

"Got one victim, male, multiple GSW," he said, pointing a thumb in the direction of the living room. "One witness, says she was upstairs. I don't know more, I just got here myself. I was visiting my folks down in Little Odessa."

"I skipped out on a family dinner," she said.

"You're welcome," he said.

She made a face. "Not everyone's family is totally screwed up."

He looked surprised. "You sure about that?"

"Where's the first responders?" she asked, changing the subject.

"We didn't need a bus," he said. "Hell, I could see that the moment I got here. The guy's as dead as I've seen."

"I mean the Patrol unit," she said. "Didn't they stick around to secure the scene?"

Vic got a funny look on his face. "Only guy when I got here was the Lieutenant."

"And that didn't strike you as strange?"

"I live in New York, Erin. I want strange, all I have to do is look out my window." He stepped out of the doorway. "C'mon in and have a look."

The living room was well furnished, but looked somehow artificial to Erin, like the interior decorator had copied it out of a picture in *Good Housekeeping*. She had a hard time imagining anyone actually living there. The sterile magazine-inspired beauty was spoiled, in any case, by the dead body sprawled on the throw rug next to the glass-topped coffee table. The dead guy looked to have been a middle-aged gentleman, clad in a white terrycloth bathrobe. The front of the robe was now deep, dark crimson and had fallen open to reveal a stout, hairy torso with at least two extra holes in its center. The man's eyes were wide open with the shock of his last moment on Earth.

Lieutenant Webb was standing by the divider that separated the living room from the dining room. He was talking to a woman who looked to be about the same age as him, but in somewhat better repair. She was pretty, a fortysomething who took care of herself. She had a pleasant face with a splash of freckles framed by brown hair with a hint of red. Erin suspected the red tint might not be entirely natural. The woman was clearly distraught. One hand was toying nervously with her hair. She was dressed like a well-to-do white-collar woman: silk blouse, professional skirt, expensive shoes. She wore no wedding ring.

"Got here as fast as I could, sir," Erin said.

"Thanks, O'Reilly," Webb said. "This is Catherine Simmons. Cath, this is Detective O'Reilly. She's our K-9 officer and my second-in-command."

Vic's face twitched slightly at that last bit, but he didn't react. After all, it was true. Erin was a Detective Second Grade, while Vic was stuck at the bottom of the Major Crimes promotion ladder.

Cath, Erin thought. Not "Ms. Simmons." All of a sudden, it hit her. She knew why no uniformed officers were here. And she knew why Webb had called her and Vic, even though they weren't on duty.

She exchanged a look with Vic and saw the same knowledge in his eyes. Webb knew the witness. There was a history there, it was obvious from the way they stood, the way they looked at one another.

The first rule of police work was very similar to the first rule of being a gangster, a lesson straight out of *The Godfather*. *It's just business, don't make it personal.*

This case was personal for Lieutenant Webb. That meant it was going to be an absolute mess. And Erin had stepped right in the middle of it.

Ready for more?

Join Steven Henry's author email list
for the latest on new releases, upcoming books and
series, behind-the-scenes details, events, and more.

Be the first to know about the next release in the
Erin O'Reilly Mysteries by signing up at
tinyurl.com/StevenHenryEmail

About the Author

Steven Henry learned how to read almost before he learned how to walk. Ever since he began reading stories, he wanted to put his own on the page. He lives a very quiet and ordinary life in Minnesota with his wife and dog.

Also by Steven Henry

Ember of Dreams
The Clarion Chronicles, Book One

When magic awakens a long-forgotten folk, a noble lady, a young apprentice, and a solitary blacksmith band together to prevent war and seek understanding between humans and elves.

Lady Kristyn Tremayne – An otherwise unremarkable young lady's open heart and inquisitive mind reveal a hidden world of magic.

Robert Blackford – A humble harp maker's apprentice dreams of being a hero.

Master Gabriel Zane – A master blacksmith's pursuit of perfection leads him to craft an enchanted sword, drawing him out of his isolation and far from his cozy home.

Lord Luthor Carnarvon – A lonely nobleman with a dark past has won the heart of Kristyn's mother, but at what cost?

Readers love *Ember of Dreams*

"The more I got to know the characters, the more I liked them. The female lead in particular is a treat to accompany on her journey from ordinary to extraordinary."

"The author's deep understanding of his protagonists' motivations and keen eye for psychological detail make Robert and his companions a likable and memorable cast."

Learn more at tinyurl.com/emberofdreams.

More great titles from Clickworks Press

www.clickworkspress.com

Hubris Towers: The Complete First Season
Ben Y. Faroe & Bill Hoard

Comedy of manners meets comedy of errors in a new series for fans of Fawlty Towers and P. G. Wodehouse.

"So funny and endearing"

"Had me laughing so hard that I had to put it down to catch my breath"

"Astoundingly, outrageously funny!"

Learn more at clickworkspress.com/hts01.

The Dream World Collective
Ben Y. Faroe

Five friends quit their jobs to chase what they love. Rent looms. Hilarity ensues.

"If you like interesting personalities, hidden depths... and hilarious dialog, this is the book for you."

"a fun, inspiring read—perfect for a sunny summer day."

"a heartwarming, feel-good story"

Learn more at clickworkspress.com/dwc.

Death's Dream Kingdom
Gabriel Blanchard

A young woman of Victorian London has been transformed into a vampire. Can she survive the world of the immortal dead—or perhaps, escape it?

"The wit and humor are as Victorian as the setting... a winsomely vulnerable and tremendously crafted work of art."

"A dramatic, engaging novel which explores themes of death, love, damnation, and redemption."

Learn more at clickworkspress.com/ddk.

Share the love!

Join our microlending team at
kiva.org/team/clickworkspress.

Keep in touch!

Join the Clickworks Press email list
and get freebies, production updates, special deals,
behind-the-scenes sneak peeks, and more.

Sign up today at clickworkspress.com/join.

9 781943 383801